Fire and Desire

G. Everleigh

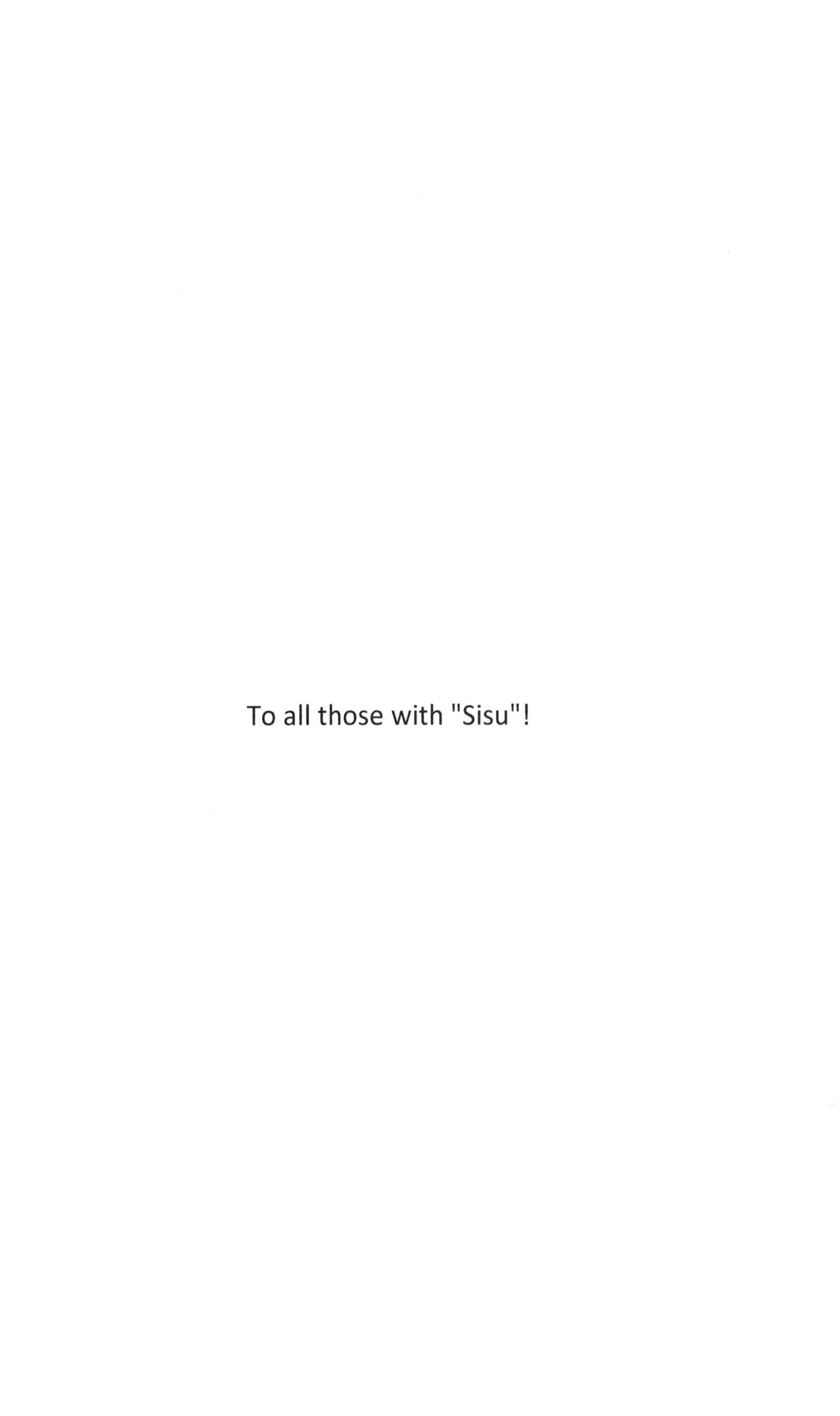

To all those with "Sisu"!

Thank you to all those who helped make this happen.

Preface

Humans and dragons have coexisted for centuries in the mystical realm of Draconia, a land steeped in rich lore and ancient history. From the towering peaks of the Dragonspire Mountains to the verdant forests of the Dragonwood, tales of bravery, magic, and adventure echo through the ages.

For generations, Draconia has been a land of peace and harmony, where humans and dragons lived side by side, bound by mutual respect and friendship. Together, they worked to protect their homeland from the forces of darkness, guided by the wisdom of the Elder Dragons, ancient beings of immense power and knowledge.

But amidst the tranquility of Draconia, whispers of a secret linger; a tale of destiny intertwined with the fate of the realm itself. And as a new chapter begins, a young girl stands on the cusp of a journey that will forever alter the course of her life and the destiny of Draconia.

Her name is yet to be known, but her story is about to unfold, a tale of courage, adventure, and the enduring bond between humans and dragons. As she sets out on her journey, she will discover secrets long buried, face challenges beyond imagination, and ultimately, learn the true meaning of bravery and sacrifice.

In the heart of Draconia, where legends are born and destinies are forged, the stage is set for a tale that will captivate the hearts and minds of all who dare to embark on this epic adventure.

Welcome to Draconia, where the bonds of friendship and the power of love hold sway over the fate of the realm.

Contents

Chapter 1: Awakening

In the enchanting realm of Draconia, where the azure sky served as a vast canvas for the majestic dragons that ruled its expanse, magic flowed like a pulsating river, meandering through the very land. The air crackled with an energy that hinted at the extraordinary as if the very breath of mythical creatures infused life into every rustling leaf and swirling eddy of wind.

A quaint cottage nestled on the outskirts of a dense forest stood as a testament to the harmony between nature and the supernatural. The trees swayed in joyous unison, their branches creating a symphony of creaks and whispers. Birds, adorned in a palette of colors unseen in the mundane world, flitted about, indulging in the bounties of nature's embrace. A cottage stood amidst this wonder and seemed almost alive, a humble haven in the heart of Draconia's wonders.

Inside, the air resonated with the melodic notes of chirping birds, their harmonies blending seamlessly with the delicate hum emanating from the young girl seated by the window. Her nimble fingers danced with purpose, a crochet hook in hand, weaving threads that mirrored the magical hues of the surrounding landscape. Her eyes sparkled with an ancient wisdom, a connection to a world beyond the veil of reality.

As she crocheted, the room appeared to respond to the pulsing cadence of her movements. A gentle breeze, not of the wind but of arcane currents, swept through the cottage, carrying with it the fragrance of unseen blossoms. Even the chirping outside transformed into a melodic chorus as if nature itself joined in the girl's creative endeavor.

The young artisan's fingers moved faster, tracing intricate patterns that mirrored the mystique of Draconia. With each loop and twist, she wove a tale into the fabric, a tale of dragons soaring through cerulean skies, of magic that whispered through the woods.

In an enchanting shift of reality, the cottage metamorphosed into a vessel of magic, seamlessly bridging the gap between the ordinary and the extraordinary. The young girl, her crochet hook choreographing an intricate dance, found herself at the nexus of this mystical alchemy, surrounded by the harmonious chorus of nature. Draconia, the ever-vigilant realm, acknowledged the homage paid by its humble resident, reciprocating with a gift of vitality that defied the constraints of imagination.

As the birds concluded their melodic performance, Saraphina set aside her own creative endeavor and erupted into applause. Her demeanor radiated joy, a vibrant acknowledgment of the feathered virtuosos. "All of you are magnificent!" she exclaimed with genuine glee, and the birds, attuned to the spirit of celebration, danced in a soft and joyful interlude.

In the midst of this quaint moment, Saraphina's jubilant expression shifted as she glanced at the time, her realization sending a jolt through her.

"Oh heavens! I needed to deliver this to Iroh! I mustn't waste time." The urgency in her voice echoed in the air, and without hesitation, she swiftly resumed her seat, determination etched on her face.

In a seamless transition, Saraphina's hands hastened, two souls drawn together a blur of swift and purposeful movements as she wove the piece with accelerated fervor. Time became an elusive companion as she poured her focus into the task, the very urgency adding a dynamic layer to the blend of creativity within the cottage.

Saraphina was a living embodiment of the symbiotic relationship between two worlds. Her existence blurred the lines between humanity and dragonhood, a bridge between the tangible and the ethereal. Born with the innate ability to seamlessly transition between her human and dragon forms, she moved through Draconia with a grace that mirrored the amicable coexistence of the creatures residing in the enchanted realm.

In human form, Saraphina was a vision of grace, her every step echoing the rhythm of Draconia's magical heartbeat. Her eyes held the depth of ancient wisdom, and her connection to the land ran as deep as the roots of the mystical trees that surrounded her cottage. When she shifted into her dragon form, she became a majestic creature, her scales reflecting the kaleidoscope of hues present in Draconia's magical landscape.

Draconia itself was a testament to the breathtaking fusion of nature and magic. Waterfalls cascaded down towering buildings constructed within colossal mountains, a surreal spectacle that blended the boundaries of reality and fantasy. Castles stretched across elongated distances, their architectural marvels standing as monuments to the enduring harmony between humans and dragons.

Within this land of wonders, a delicate balance existed. Humans and dragons coexisted not as separate entities but as interconnected threads in the vast tapestry of Draconia's existence. Saraphina, with her unique ability to traverse both worlds, served as a living symbol of this unity. Her humble cottage, nestled on the outskirts, became a sanctuary where the magical and mundane intersected seamlessly.

Saraphina kept her true nature hidden from the world; a secret nestled deep within the chambers of her heart. The shift between her human and dragon forms was a delicate secret concealed beneath the veil of normalcy.

The consequence of unveiling her secret loomed like a shadow in Saraphina's thoughts. The harmony between humans and dragons was a fragile balance, and the revelation of her dual nature could disrupt the tranquility of Draconia. Fear coiled within her, an ancient instinct urging caution, as she navigated the intricate web of relationships and alliances that defined the enchanted realm.

As her hands continued the swift ballet with the crochet hook, Saraphina stole a glance at the window where the birds had lingered moments ago. Their freedom in flight, unburdened by the need for secrecy, sparked a yearning within her. The desire to soar through the skies in her true form, to unleash the majestic dragon within, warred with the fear of potential repercussions.

The fading echoes of the birds' wings carried with them the melancholy reminder of the freedom Saraphina craved, a longing that had to remain veiled beneath layers of secrecy. Her eyes, reflective of her complex emotions, flitted between the window and the completed creation. The threads she wove mirrored the intertwining strands of her own desires and the reality she was bound to uphold. Yet, in the depths of her gaze, determination remained steadfast, a silent vow to preserve the delicate equilibrium she had maintained so far.

As Saraphina finished the last stitch, a triumphant smile graced her lips. Her gaze lingered on the crocheted sweater, a tangible manifestation of her artistic prowess and a symbol of the unspoken bond she shared with her dear friend, Iroh. Their connection stretched back to Saraphina's infancy as a dragon, abandoned and vulnerable in the depths of a cave system that Iroh used to mine for gems and quartzes. It was Iroh who discovered her, a serendipitous encounter that forged a lifelong friendship.

With the completed sweater cradled in her arms, pride and joy radiated through Saraphina. It was a gift, not merely a physical garment, but a token of gratitude and love for the one who had been there from the beginning.

The urgency to deliver her creation propelled Saraphina into swift action. Clicking her feet on the wooden floor, she stepped out of the cottage into the embrace of Draconia's ambient magic. Under her breath, she whispered ancient incantations, words that resonated with the essence of the enchanted realm.

"Oh Grande Draconia, accorde-moi la sagesse!"

As the whispered words hung in the air, a subtle transformation began. The air shimmered around Saraphina, and her form shifted, her human exterior blending seamlessly with her true dragon nature. Feathers emerged, delicate scales glistened, and wings unfolded with grace, casting a spectral glow around her. In moments, Saraphina had transformed into a majestic dragon, ready to traverse the skies.

The wind whispered secrets as Saraphina took flight, her silhouette disappearing into the azure canvas of Draconia's sky. She soared through the skies, her wings cutting through the currents of Draconia's enchanting atmosphere. The grandeur of Draconia stretched out before her, a panorama of breathtaking beauty.

The prominent beat of her wings echoed the pulsating energy of the land, and as Saraphina embraced her true form, a sense of liberation washed over her. The longing in her eyes transformed into a radiant sparkle, and the vast expanse of the sky became her canvas. She circled above the mountains, reveling in the freedom she had temporarily reclaimed.

As Saraphina approached Iroh's dwelling, memories flooded her mind. Iroh, a steadfast caretaker who had taken her in when she was but a baby dragon, had played a pivotal role in shaping her understanding of Draconia's wonders. The bond they shared was a testament to the interconnectedness of beings in this mystical realm.

Descending gracefully, Saraphina's large wings folded as she landed near Iroh's home. With a shimmering burst of magic, her dragon form transitioned seamlessly back into her human self. She stood before Iroh's door with the crocheted sweater cradled in her arms.

Iroh, an elderly man with a kind demeanor and a twinkle in his eye, greeted Saraphina with a warm smile. "Ah, Saraphina, my dear. What brings you here today?"

Saraphina, still in awe of the transformation she had just undergone, presented the crocheted sweater with a grin. "I made this for you, Iroh. A token of appreciation for all you've done for me."

Iroh's eyes twinkled with gratitude as he accepted the gift. "You've grown into a remarkable young woman, Saraphina. Draconia has been kind to us both."

The rest of the afternoon was spent sharing stories and laughter. Saraphina finally bid farewell to Iroh as the sun dipped below the horizon. The secret she carried within remained safeguarded, but the moments of freedom in her true form were a testament to the resilience of her spirit. With a final glance back at the cottage, Saraphina took flight once again, disappearing into the night sky, where the echoes of Draconia's magic lingered in the stars.

Chapter 2: A Fateful Encounter

The first rays of dawn bathed Saraphina's cottage in a soft, golden glow as she moved with purpose in the kitchen. The aroma of fresh herbs and spices filled the air as she deftly prepared a feast fit for a celebration. Today was no ordinary day; it was Iroh's birthday, and Saraphina was determined to express her gratitude in the most special way possible.

A symphony of culinary creativity echoed through the cozy kitchen — the sizzling of pans, the chopping of vegetables, and the gentle hum of an ancient Draconian melody playing in the background created a pleasant ambiance. Saraphina's culinary skills were as enchanting as her crocheting, and she poured her heart into each dish, infusing them with the magic of Draconia itself.

As the delicious aroma of the food being prepared filled her quaint abode, Saraphina couldn't help but reminisce about the times when Iroh had rescued her from the encaving's depths. His kindness and care had been a guiding light in her life, and she owed him more than words could convey.

The table, adorned with vibrant Draconian flowers and flickering candles, awaited Iroh's arrival. Saraphina took a moment to appreciate the effort she had put into making everything perfect. A crocheted table runner adorned with intricate patterns added a touch of her artistic flair to the scene.

As the clock ticked closer to the lunch, a knock on the door announced Iroh's arrival. Saraphina greeted him with a warm smile, her eyes sparkling with excitement.

"Happy birthday, Iroh! Today, I've prepared something special."

Iroh, touched by the gesture, entered the cottage, his eyes widening at the sight of the beautifully set table. The air was filled with the enticing aroma of the carefully crafted meal, and the Draconian melody swirled around them, adding to the enchantment of the moment.

The lunch unfolded as a celebration of friendship, with laughter and heartfelt conversations weaving through each bite. Saraphina, with each glance exchanged and each shared story felt a profound sense of gratitude for the bonds that connected them in the magical realm of Draconia.

Amidst the festivities, Iroh spoke of ancient ruins nestled within the steep mountains of Draconia, a topic that piqued Saraphina's interest. He revealed tales of a great treasure hidden within these ruins, a revelation that ignited a spark of excitement in her. Intrigued by the prospect, especially considering her penchant for wandering into the mountains during her alone time, Saraphina listened intently.

After lunch, Iroh took his leave, and Saraphina was left alone with her thoughts. The seed of curiosity had taken root in her mind. Obsessed with the idea of uncovering this treasure, she decided to embark on the journey to the ruins the next morning.

The dawn cast its soft glow over Draconia as Saraphina, fueled by a mixture of anticipation and determination, ventured into the mountains. Finding the ancient ruins proved to be a straightforward task, as if the land itself guided her steps. Yet, the true challenge lay in unraveling the secrets hidden deep within the corridors of the ruins, where shadows whispered tales of a treasure waiting to be discovered.

Days melted into a continuous stream of exploration, and Saraphina's quest for the elusive treasure seemed to be an endless journey. Despite her relentless efforts, the hidden chambers of the ruins held no trace of riches. The dusty corridors, ancient and mysterious, echoed with the footsteps of a determined dragon shifter who refused to succumb to disappointment.

Undeterred, Saraphina delved deeper, her senses attuned to the secrets that lingered within the stone walls. Her search evolved from a pursuit of treasure to a fascination with the artifacts and gemstones that adorned the ruins. With each passing day, the ruins revealed fragments of their history— antiques, intricate carvings, and precious stones, each telling a tale of a bygone era.

Saraphina's perseverance finally bore fruit when she stumbled upon a rugged path hidden within the depths of the ruins. A path less trodden, whispering promises of discovery. With a deep breath, she ventured onto the narrow trail, guided by an instinct that had kept her spirits alive through the arduous journey.

The cave that unfolded before her was a revelation. Crystals glistened in the dim light, embedded within the stone like nature's own treasure chest. Raw emeralds and quartzes adorned the cave walls, casting a radiant glow that illuminated the cavern. Saraphina stood in awe, her eyes reflecting the brilliance of the precious stones that surrounded her.

The treasure she sought was not gold or silver but the untold beauty of the earth itself. The cave, a sanctuary of raw gemstones, held a value far beyond material riches. Each glimmering crystal told a story of ancient forces, of the mystical energy that coursed through Draconia's veins.

At that moment, Saraphina felt a profound connection with the land she called home. With a sense of fulfillment, she marveled at the raw beauty surrounding her, a testament to the rewards that awaited those who ventured deep into the heart of the enchanted realm.

Saraphina wasted no time; she took flight, her wings slicing through the air as she soared toward Iroh's dwelling. Within moments, she arrived, excitement radiating from her as she burst through the door to share her newfound treasure with her dear friend.

"Iroh! Iroh!" she exclaimed, her eyes sparkling with the joy of discovery. "You won't believe what I found in the depths of the ruins!"

Iroh looked up from his contemplative state, a curious twinkle in his eyes. "What is it, Saraphina? What has you so elated?"

With animated gestures, Saraphina described the cave adorned with raw emeralds and quartzes, her words painting a vivid picture of the natural treasure trove hidden within Draconia's ancient ruins. Iroh listened intently, his eyes widening with each detail.

"An entire cave filled with raw gemstones?" he marveled. "Truly, this is a discovery worth celebrating!"

As the realization of Saraphina's revelation sank in, joy erupted between them. The room transformed into a dance floor, and they twirled in celebration, their laughter echoing the shared exhilaration of this extraordinary find. The treasure, once shrouded in mystery, had become a source of boundless joy.

After the impromptu dance of celebration, Iroh and Saraphina exchanged knowing glances. "We must explore this cave further," Iroh suggested, his voice filled with enthusiasm. "Such wonders should not be kept to ourselves."

Saraphina nodded in agreement. "And I would love for you to witness the beauty of the cave firsthand. It's a magical place, Iroh, and I want to share it with you."

The decision was made, and Saraphina and Iroh found themselves planning regular visits to the newfound cave. What was once a hidden gem evolved into a shared sanctuary, a place where the raw beauty of gemstones intertwined with the camaraderie of kindred spirits. Saraphina, imbued with the spirit of generosity, extended the invitation not only to Iroh but to her animal companions as well—avian friends and creatures native to Draconia.

The cave, once shrouded in secrecy, transformed into a haven of shared joy and discovery. Each visit became a celebration of friendship, where the flickering glow of raw gemstones illuminated the faces of those who marveled at the enchanting wonders within the ancient walls.

As the seasons unfolded, a new chapter began in Saraphina's life. One day, while exploring the ancient ruins of Draconia, she felt a magnetic pull drawing her deeper into the corridors. The air, thick with the whispers of time, carried an unspoken invitation that she couldn't ignore.

As if guided by an invisible force, Saraphina sensed the presence of another within the ruins. Following an instinct she couldn't explain, she turned a corner to discover a man, battered and wounded, lying among the ancient stones. His armor told tales of battles fought, and his eyes, though weary, held a spark of resilience. Intrigued by the magnetic force that had led her to him, Saraphina approached the man, her heart beating in rhythm with the echoes of the ruins.

Without uttering a word, she began tending to his wounds with a skill that seemed second nature to her. The air around them shimmered with an ethereal energy as Saraphina's healing touch worked its magic. The man, initially surprised by her sudden appearance, soon found solace in the warmth of her presence.

As Saraphina nursed him back to health, a silent understanding formed between them—a connection that transcended the ordinary encounters of Draconia. Unaware of the profound impact this meeting would have on her life, Saraphina continued her ministrations, the ruins standing witness to the unfolding destinies of two souls drawn together by forces beyond their comprehension.

The man looked at her with a mixture of gratitude and curiosity.

"Who are you?" he asked, his voice echoing through the ancient chamber.

"I am Saraphina, a native of Draconia," she replied, her eyes holding a wisdom that belied her youthful appearance.

"And who might you be?" She inquired as she looked at his wounds, briefly enchanted by the physical appearance of the man.

Elian's gaze lingered on Saraphina, his eyes reflecting something he had never seen before. The ancient chamber seemed to pulse with unseen energy as the two shared a moment of unspoken connection.

"Draconia," Elian echoed, a hint of recognition in his eyes. "A land of mystery and enchantment. I've heard tales of its wonders, but never did I imagine encountering one of its inhabitants."

Saraphina, sensing the curiosity in Elian's voice, offered a gentle smile. "Draconia's magic flows like a river, and dragons soar through the skies. It's a land that holds ancient secrets and timeless wonders. A land I call home."

Elian, still absorbing the surreal nature of the encounter, propped himself up on his elbows. "And what brings you to these ancient ruins, Saraphina?"

The air around them hummed with an unspoken understanding as if the ruins themselves were witnesses to the unfolding tale of their meeting. Saraphina's gaze softened, revealing a depth of emotion as she spoke.

"I felt a pull that led me here. The ruins whispered to me, drawing me to you," she explained, her words carrying a weight that transcended the confines of the ancient chamber.

Elian, intrigued by the mystique of Draconia and captivated by Saraphina's presence, nodded in quiet acknowledgment. "Perhaps there's a reason our paths have crossed in this sacred place."

After their profound conversation, Saraphina, with gentle care, helped Elian rise to his feet. Together, they navigated through the cave toward the mountain top, the gemstone-laden walls bearing silent witness to their journey. Confusion marked Saraphina's expression as she questioned Elian about the circumstances that led him to this mystical realm.

"How did you end up here again?" she inquired, her eyes searching his. Elian chuckled softly before responding, "I frankly do not remember, miss. All I know is I fell from a huge mountain and ended up being tended to by you."

Saraphina smiled, intrigued by the mystery that surrounded Elian's arrival. "Where would you like to go, Mister Elian?"

"Home, presumably," he replied, his gaze wandering into the distance.

"In this condition? I suggest you rest at my house for a few days; your wounds have not properly healed. And wherever home is, I don't think you'd know your way around here," Saraphina suggested with a happy demeanor.

"Well, you're not wrong about that," Elian chuckled, appreciating the warmth of Saraphina's hospitality. However, a practical concern crossed his mind. "But how are we going to get down from here?"

"Um... would you mind waiting here for a moment? I'll fetch someone who can assist us," Saraphina hesitated, cautious about revealing her secret identity at this point.

"Pardon my curiosity, but how do you plan to descend a steep mountain?" Elian raised an eyebrow, peering down the slope.

"Just wait, okay!" Saraphina gestured downward toward the cave's location, signaling her bird friends with a whistle. After a brief wait, Phil, a majestic eagle, arrived at her call.

"Ah, Phil! I can't believe it worked! No time to explain, though. I need you to summon Iroh at the mountain's summit; someone needs our help. Be quick!" Saraphina directed Phil, who chirped and flapped his wings, soaring toward Iroh's location.

While Phil carried out the message, Saraphina made her way back to the mountain's top and sat down with Elian.

"So?" Elian inquired, tilting his head in confusion.

"Now we wait! I've asked Phil to come and help us," Saraphina replied cheerfully.

"Phil?"

"Yeah, my friend, the eagle," she smiled, continuing the conversation.

"You can talk to birds?" Elian asked, astonished yet intrigued.

"Yeah, I can! Everyone in Draconia can talk to birds!" Saraphina blurted out, realizing she had momentarily let her secret slip. However, she swiftly regained her composure, avoiding any suspicion.

In the meantime, Iroh arrived in a carriage carried by a bird-like dragon. Its majestic wings facilitated the descent of the carriage, and Iroh settled atop the mountain, startling Elian.

"WHAT IS THAT?!" he exclaimed.

"Ah, you must be new here. This is Ellis, the Roaming Dragon," Iroh responded with a chuckle.

"A dragon?!" Elian panicked visibly, reassured by Saraphina, who held his hand and smiled.

"Calm down, Ellis is very friendly. She's a sweetheart; I'll show you!" Saraphina reached out to pet Ellis's beak, and the dragon squawked happily, lowering its head for Saraphina's hug.

"I missed you! Where have you been?" Saraphina inquired, her face glowing with joy.

Elian was left stunned by the sight of people and dragons being friends, even companions. The unexpected bond between humans and dragons unfolded before him, shattering preconceived notions. Elian's astonishment grew as he witnessed the heartfelt connection between Saraphina and Ellis. It was a scene unlike anything he had experienced in his world, where dragons were often feared and considered dangerous creatures. Saraphina, sensing Elian's bewilderment, explained with a warm smile.

"In Draconia, dragons and humans share a unique bond. We understand each other, and many of us have companions like Ellis here. They're not just powerful creatures; they're friends, protectors, and allies," Saraphina spoke as she smiled.

Elian settled into the carriage, feeling a mix of excitement and trepidation. Saraphina's infectious enthusiasm and Iroh's calm reassurance began to ease his nerves. As the carriage door closed, Saraphina couldn't contain her delight.

"You're gonna love this!" Iroh, standing outside the carriage, closed the door with a knowing smile.

"You guys might want to buckle up or hold onto something," he suggested, a hint of amusement in his voice. With that, Ellis spread her magnificent wings and, with a powerful flap, lifted off the ground.

The sensation of soaring through the air was exhilarating, and Elian marveled at the breathtaking scenery unfolding below. The wind whistled past the carriage as Ellis navigated the skies with grace. Saraphina, sensing Elian's awe, couldn't resist sharing more about their incredible journey.

"Isn't this amazing? Ellis can take us anywhere we want in Draconia. The view is always spectacular!" Saraphina grinned, enjoying Elian's wide-eyed wonder.

Elian, despite his initial apprehension, found himself enchanted by the magic of the airborne adventure. The landscape below shifted, revealing lush forests, sparkling rivers, and towering mountains. It was a sight beyond anything he could have imagined.

As Ellis gracefully descended toward their destination, Iroh prepared Elian for the landing. "Hold on tight; we're almost there," he advised, and Elian braced himself for the descent. The Roaming Dragon descended with precision, gently touching down on a landing platform in Draconia's heart.

The carriage door opened, revealing the vibrant surroundings of the magical realm. Saraphina, with a beaming smile, extended a hand to Elian.

"This is where I live," Saraphina showed him her cozy cottage. As they entered Saraphina's home, she offered Elian a comfortable seat. The atmosphere was infused with warmth and the subtle hum of Draconia's magic, creating a haven where tales of the past and dreams of the future converged.

Over the next few days, Elian rested and recovered under Saraphina's care. Their conversations delved into the mysteries of Draconia, the enchantments that defined the land, and the uncharted territories that awaited discovery. The bond between them grew stronger, weaving a connection that extended beyond the ordinary realms of friendship.

As they shared stories and laughter, Elian found himself drawn to Saraphina's wisdom and the allure of Draconia's wonders. The fateful meeting within the ancient ruins had not only led him to a place of healing but had also opened the door to a realm of possibilities he could never have imagined.

Little did they know that their journey had just begun. The echoes of Draconia's magic resonated in the air, whispering of adventures yet to unfold and destinies yet to be unveiled. Saraphina and Elian stood at the crossroads of the ordinary and the extraordinary, ready to embark on a path that would reshape the tapestry of their lives in ways they could scarcely fathom.

Chapter 3: Forbidden Desires

The sun's golden rays bathed Draconia in a warm embrace as a new day unfurled its wings. The sweet melodies of birdsong filled the air, and Saraphina, with her hair tousled and eyes still heavy with sleep, embraced the familiar routine of waking up to Phil and his friends' cheerful chirps.

"Good morning! How are you, Phil?" Saraphina's joyful greeting echoed through the room. Phil and his feathery companions responded with an orchestrated chorus of tweets. Saraphina's infectious happiness seemed to lift the spirits of the avian ensemble.

As she stretched and sang along with the birds, her attention turned to Phil, and a playful suggestion formed on her lips. "How is Elian, you ask? Why don't you go wake him up?"

With a mischievous gleam in his eye, Phil darted from Saraphina's room into the chamber where Elian was still resting. He perched on Elian's forehead, pecking gently and chirping until Elian stirred from his slumber.

"Huh?" Elian groggily woke up, rubbing his forehead. The room was empty, and he dismissed the unusual wake-up call as a fleeting dream. "Must be dreaming, I guess. Oh well."

Just as he settled back to sleep, Saraphina entered the room, her wet hair clinging to her pale skin. Dressed in a simple black cottage dress, she exuded an ethereal charm that captivated Elian's attention, and he sat right up. She noticed his gaze, and with a flick of her fingers, she playfully brought him back to the present.

"You want breakfast?" Saraphina's smile was warm and inviting, dismissing any lingering traces of awkwardness. Trying to regain composure, Elian stammered, "Y-yeah, Yeah. Ahem," and quickly diverted his eyes, making his way to the restroom.

As Elian stood in front of the mirror, he couldn't help but reflect on the changing dynamics between him and Saraphina. The more time they spent together, the more he found himself drawn to her infectious energy and the enchanting world of Draconia. The newfound fondness in his heart was evident, and he couldn't deny the subtle magic that had woven its way into their shared moments.

The days unfolded in a harmonious rhythm for Saraphina and Elian, a symphony of shared moments and discoveries that laid the foundation of their growing bond. Saraphina's culinary talents became a delightful constant in their routine, each meal a testament to her warmth and care.

"Do you like it? I made it myself," Saraphina beamed as she waited for Elian to say something as he took a bite of the dish she had crafted with love.

Elian's eyes lit up with genuine delight, and he exclaimed between mouthfuls, "You are extraordinary, Saraphina. This is amazing!" His childlike enthusiasm brought a radiant smile to Saraphina's face, and she couldn't help but feel a deep sense of satisfaction.

"I'm glad you love it!" Saraphina giggled with joy as she replenished Elian's bowl. She stole a secret glance at him, taking in the sight of him savoring the meal she had prepared so lovingly for him. The more he ate, the more her happiness swelled, not just from the appreciation of her cooking but from witnessing his gradual recovery and well-being.

As Elian's wounds healed, their bond of friendship grew stronger. They explored the ancient ruins together, unearthing stones and antique artifacts that whispered tales of Draconia's past. Saraphina, with her skillful hands, transformed these discoveries into intricate jewelry and necklaces, tangible reminders of their shared adventures.

The evenings were filled with laughter, stories, and the echoes of Draconia's magic. They would sit by the fire, sharing tales of their respective worlds and dreams.

Elian spoke of his past, his adventures, and the life he led before stumbling upon Draconia.

"I used to be a merchant in the city of Astoria," he started, his eyes reflecting a mix of nostalgia and pain. "I dealt in rare artifacts and gems, and my reputation was on the rise."

Saraphina listened attentively as Elian continued, "But then, false allegations of bribery stained my name. I had no say in it, but who could ever fight the government?" His voice carried a weight of injustice, laden with the echoes of a past that had led him to Draconia.

"I was exiled from Astoria and branded a criminal without a chance to defend myself. So, I became a wanderer. I had a few coins of my fortune left and just the will to keep going. Out in the wandering wilds, not everyone is exactly your friend."

"You have to fend for yourself, fend for your belongings. I had to learn how to fight from a few wandering freedom fighters who were exiled from Astoria on unjust terms; they molded me into a warrior. I outclassed every other looter with ease," he continued.

"It all led me into a really big trap. A few looters gathered around me and outnumbered me. That's how I got this shoulder wound," Elian lifted his shirt to show it to her. "I remember I was on the brink of exhaustion, barely escaping, if I might add, and I saw a waterfall. The moment I drank from that, I was caught by poachers who wanted the coins I had left."

"And then they used force...!" Elian exclaimed, continuing, "Yes, the wounds were very brash, and to escape, I jumped into the waterfall as a last-ditch effort. The last thing I remember is landing in that cave at the end of the waterfall."

Saraphina's eyes filled with empathy for Elian's past ordeal, and she spoke softly, "I'm so sorry." She reached out and gently held his hand on her own. The warmth of her touch was calming and consoling, deepening their connection as he shared the painful chapters of his life.

As Saraphina held his hand, Elian felt a sense of comfort, a reassurance that he had found a true friend in this mystical realm. Saraphina, curious yet gentle, redirected the conversation to brighter memories, asking, "What were your most cherished memories as a merchant?"

Elian's eyes softened, and a nostalgic smile played on his lips. "The bustling markets, the joy of discovering rare treasures, and the art of knowing when to compromise. There was a thrill in each trade. My most cherished memories were the moments when someone's face lit up upon finding the perfect artifact, a piece of history they could hold."

Saraphina smiled, captivated by Elian's tales. "Your love for treasures is inspiring. Draconia has its own wonders to offer. I was in that cave to uncover them for myself, but now that I think about it, I feel as if we can do it together."

Elian's smile mirrored hers as he replied, "I look forward to exploring the mysteries of Draconia with you, Saraphina."

Feeling a surge of warmth, Saraphina stood up, holding Elian in her arms. Her eyes radiated reassurance as she spoke, "You're safe here, Elian. Trust me."

They shared a warm hug, a gesture that transcended words and deepened the heartfelt connection between her and the exiled merchant.

***

As the dinner hour approached, Iroh extended a warm invitation to Saraphina and Elian to join him for a celebratory meal after their day at the ruins. The prospect of a delightful evening filled with good company and hearty food was enticing, but Elian found himself facing a dilemma—he had nothing suitable to wear for such an occasion.

Saraphina, ever resourceful and mischievous, decided to remedy the situation by borrowing some clothes from Iroh. "Here, Iroh was roughly the same height as yours in his youth," she said, handing Elian a few shirts.

Gratefully, Elian accepted the garments, taking his time to change. Meanwhile, Saraphina transformed herself for the special dinner, adorning a lovely dress. Little did Elian know, it was not just any dinner—it was Saraphina's birthday.

As Elian entered the room, his appearance left Saraphina utterly stunned. The white flair shirt complemented his olive skin, and an amethyst necklace adorned his neck, accentuating his natural beauty. Elian, in his late twenties, possessed a broad frame that carried the shirt with grace. Saraphina couldn't take her eyes off him as he casually dried his hair and pulled it back with a comb.

Lost in the moment, Saraphina stole glances at Elian, her heart beating faster with every subtle movement he made. Unbeknownst to Elian, he had become the inadvertent focal point of her attention, and the air between them seemed charged with a newfound energy.

"Sara? Are you okay?" Elian's voice broke through Saraphina's reverie as he stood in front of her, towering over her smaller frame. "You look pale. Are you okay?"

Startled, Saraphina stammered, taken aback by sudden questioning, "Oh? Me? Yes, I'm fine, heh." Her cheeks flushed with embarrassment, and she looked away, adding finishing touches to her attire. Elian sensed a tension in the air but chose to remain silent, not wanting to intrude or make the situation awkward.

Finally ready, Elian turned toward Saraphina, his eyes catching hers in an unspoken exchange. "Shall we?" he gestured toward the door, breaking the momentary silence.

Saraphina, collecting herself, nodded with a soft smile. "Yes, let's go."

The dinner at Iroh's was no ordinary affair. The atmosphere buzzed with warmth and laughter as Saraphina, Elian, and Iroh shared stories, delicious food, and the camaraderie of newfound friendships. The table was adorned with gems and luxurious items they had discovered during their recent ventures into the ruins, adding an extra layer of magic to the celebration.

As the evening progressed, Iroh raised his glass for a toast. "To Saraphina, and to Elian, the newest addition to our adventurous family. May Draconia continue to bless us with treasures and shared moments."

Glasses clinked, and laughter filled the room as they celebrated not just the discoveries of the ruins but the bonds that had formed between them. Saraphina couldn't help but steal glances at Elian, her heart swelling with gratitude for the presence of this unexpected companion in her life.

As the party music reverberated throughout the rooms, Iroh invited a few friends of Saraphina to aid the atmosphere, and all of them enjoyed the night away. Amidst the dancing and laughter, Saraphina caught sight of Elian standing alone in the backyard of the house, gazing up at the stars. She decided to approach him, his solitary figure beckoning her curiosity.

"Hey, what are you doing here all alone?" Saraphina asked, leaning on the railing beside him.

"Oh, I'm just watching the stars. They look much clearer than they did in Astoria," Elian replied, his gaze shifting from the sky to meet hers, welcoming her with a soft smile.

Under the canopy of Draconia's stars, Saraphina and Elian shared a quiet moment, the air filled with the whispers of magic.

As they stargazed, the conversation naturally flowed, and Saraphina began to share fragments of her mysterious origin.

"Iroh has been my mother and father. I don't remember who my real parents were, but he never made me question them. He took care of me like his own, and all the kindness in my heart is because of the love he gave me as a child," Saraphina confessed, a soft tear glistening in her eyes.

Elian, sensing the sensitivity of the topic, reached out and tenderly wiped her tears away. A smile played on his lips as she looked beautiful, even with tears in her eyes.

"I know what it's like to be an orphan. My parents left me at the age of five, and even though I tried to find them, it only brought guilt for not utilizing that time to find myself," Elian shared, his voice filled with empathy.

Saraphina's heart swelled with compassion as she listened, realizing the depth of Elian's own past struggles. She placed her hand over his on her cheek, her touch a silent gesture of solidarity.

"I could never relate to the extent of heartbreak you felt, but I am so glad you had someone like Iroh in your life. You deserve him, and he deserves a daughter like you," Elian whispered, caressing her cheek.

At that moment, their vulnerabilities met, and without a word, Saraphina leaned in and tenderly kissed Elian's lips. He was momentarily startled, but as the gravity of the moment sunk in, they shared a tender kiss, the tension between them melting away.

The entire night unfolded in a symphony of intimacy and shared moments at Iroh's party, but the growing closeness between Saraphina and Elian started to raise a subtle unease in Iroh's mind. He harbored a deep concern that the secrets Saraphina held, especially her true nature as a dragon shifter, could be at risk of revelation.

Deciding to leave the party early, Saraphina and Elian escaped into the night, their connection only deepening as they ventured toward Saraphina's home. Iroh's watchful gaze lingered on them, worry etched on his features. The need to protect Saraphina's secrets weighed heavily on him.

As soon as they reached her cottage, the atmosphere became charged with an undeniable electricity. Saraphina latched onto Elian, their lips meeting in tender kisses. The world outside disappeared as they closed the door behind them, retreating into the cocoon of their shared space.

Amidst the sweet and passionate moments, Saraphina whispered, "This is the best birthday gift ever," her words resonating with a joy that transcended the ordinary. Elian chuckled, showering her with love that echoed through the night.

The warmth of Draconia wrapped around them like a protective cloak, but little did they know that their blissful night also carried with it the weight of untold secrets. Iroh, torn between the desire for Saraphina's happiness and the need to safeguard her hidden identity, watched over them from afar, his concern a silent undercurrent beneath the surface of their shared joy.

***

The next morning unfolded with the soft glow of dawn, and Saraphina and Elian found themselves waking up in each other's embrace. Tender pecks and kisses showered upon them, creating a lingering warmth that filled the room. After a shared breakfast, they sat down to continue their conversations, weaving together stories of Astoria and Draconia.

As the fatigue from the previous night settled in, Saraphina nestled into her bed, and Elian, understanding her need for rest, decided to explore the ruins on his own.

Hours later, Iroh knocked on Saraphina's door, his expression carrying a weight of concern. Seated next to her, he spoke to her about Elian.

"You really seem to be drawn to this man, Saraphina," Iroh stated, his gaze penetrating yet filled with concern. "Are you sure you can trust him?"

Saraphina met his gaze with unwavering determination. "Yes, I am very sure, Iroh. I truly like him a lot, and we have shared many meaningful moments these past few weeks."

Iroh's expression softened, a subtle mixture of understanding and apprehension crossing his features. "My child, you know I have never told you to put your brakes on anything, right? You're a free bird; you deserve to keep soaring, but you must remember, as a dragon shifter, loving a human is strictly forbidden."

Saraphina nodded; her heart heavy with the weight of Iroh's words.

"I know, Iroh, but..."

"You also know the consequences of your actions?" Iroh interjected, weariness etched in his features as he gently held her hands in his own.

Saraphina remained silent, her head dipped in a mix of turmoil and contemplation. Her fingers unconsciously fiddled with the fabric of her shirt, a physical manifestation of the inner conflict raging within her.

"Just be careful, okay?" Iroh sighed, his voice laced with a blend of paternal concern and solemn warning. He tenderly caressed her cheek, his touch a silent reassurance amidst the storm of emotions swirling around them. "I don't want you getting into trouble."

"I'll try my best, Iroh. Thank you so much for always being here," Saraphina replied, her voice filled with a mixture of gratitude and affection. The unspoken bond between them, forged through years of shared experiences and unwavering support, resonated with a depth that transcended the ordinary.

In the quiet embrace of Draconia, where magic and forbidden love danced on the delicate threads of fate, Saraphina faced the daunting realities of her existence. The echoes of Iroh's warning lingered in the air, a constant reminder of the tightrope she walked between love and duty and the need to navigate the treacherous waters of forbidden desires.

Chapter 4: Secrets Unveiled

Days slipped away like sand through the fingers of time as Saraphina, burdened by the weight of responsibility and a deep-seated fear of consequences, chose to maintain a calculated distance from Elian. The reminder of the forbidden relationship between a human and a dragon shifter had cast a shadow over their budding connection.

The vibrant moments they once shared seemed to dissolve into the background, replaced by a tentative hesitation that lingered in the air. Saraphina's decision to pull away was not rooted in a lack of affection but rather a profound understanding of the potential repercussions. She did not want to disappoint Iroh, a father figure whose care and wisdom had guided her throughout her existence. Not only that, she harbored a deep concern for Elian's well-being, and being fully aware of the power wielded by the Council of Dragons, she knew he would be in trouble if their relationship was exposed.

The days stretched on, and Saraphina, torn between her own desires and the duty ingrained in her by Draconia's rules, grappled with the internal conflict that threatened to unravel the fragile threads connecting her to Elian.

Elian, perceptive to the palpable shift, struggled to comprehend the cause of this sudden change. His attempts to engage Saraphina in conversation were met with curt responses or a stoic silence that seemed to widen the emotional gap between them. The warmth that had once radiated from their shared moments now seemed like a distant memory.

During one of their meals, as the silence persisted, Elian decided to address the unspoken rift. "Saraphina, we used to talk, laugh, and share so much. What happened to us?" he asked, his eyes searching hers for a glimmer of understanding.

Saraphina, torn between the desire to explain and the weight of the unspoken truth, hesitated before responding. "Elian, it's complicated. I just... I need to figure things out."

Elian's face betrayed a mixture of frustration and hurt. "So, you're just going to avoid me? Pretend like we never had something real?"

Saraphina, unable to meet his gaze, mumbled, "It's for your safety, Elian. I can't risk anything happening to you."

Feeling a wave of conflicting emotions, Elian decided to play along with her silence, realizing that pushing her might only make things worse. He masked his frustration with forced nonchalance, responding with a casual tone that belied the turmoil within. "Fine, Saraphina. If that's what you need, I'll give you the space you want."

As Elian left the room, the weight of his departing footsteps seemed to echo the heaviness in Saraphina's heart. Alone in the quiet of their shared space, she felt the suffocating grip of grief and guilt tightening around her.

Tears welled up in her eyes as she grappled with the conflicting emotions swirling within her. She wanted nothing more than to reach out to Elian, to hold him close and confess the depth of her feelings. But the specter of danger loomed large, casting a shadow over their budding romance.

With a heavy sigh, Saraphina bowed her head, her heart heavy with the burden of responsibility. She couldn't risk Elian's safety for the sake of her own feelings. No matter how much it pained her to do so, she knew that keeping her distance was the only way to protect him.

***

The shared adventures that had once been the cornerstone of their relationship had now become solitary endeavors, each venturing into the depths of the cave alone, their discoveries shrouded in secrecy. Saraphina's heart ached with every precious gem she unearthed, longing to share the joy of her findings with Elian. Yet, the fear of endangering him kept her silent.

Similarly, Elian's heart grew heavy with every hidden artifact he stumbled upon; his excitement tempered by the knowledge that sharing his discoveries with Saraphina would only serve to widen the chasm between them. Despite his curiosity about what had transpired between them, he chose to bury his questions beneath a facade of indifference, unwilling to pry into Saraphina's guarded secrets.

As the days stretched into weeks, their interactions became mere echoes of what they once were, the warmth of their shared moments replaced by an icy distance that seemed insurmountable.

Yet, beneath the surface, the embers of their love still smoldered a flicker of hope amidst the darkness that threatened to engulf them. With every passing day, Saraphina and Elian grappled with the silent anguish of their separation, longing for a way to bridge the chasm that divided them. But for now, they remained trapped in a cycle of solitude and silence, their hearts yearning for a connection that seemed just out of reach.

One day, Saraphina could not take it anymore. She rushed out of the house and soared into the sky in her dragon form as she made her way to Iroh's dwelling in angst and anxiety. Little did she know Elian was nearby, returning from his tiring day at the cave. He noticed the dragon soaring into the sky, and he looked at it peculiarly.

The dragon had an ember pink shade mixed with purples and reds, which were the colors Saraphina normally wore. Instinctively, he started following the dragon, his curiosity growing with each passing moment. He couldn't shake the feeling that there was something familiar about the creature soaring gracefully through the sky. The vibrant hues of pink, purple, and red that adorned its scales seemed to stir a distant memory within him, tugging at the corners of his consciousness.

With each beat of its powerful wings, the dragon drew closer to a familiar place, which Elian realized was Iroh's dwelling, its path unwavering as if driven by an unseen force. Elian followed, his steps quickening with a sense of urgency he couldn't quite explain.

As they approached the small cottage Iroh called home, Elian's heart raced with anticipation. He couldn't shake the feeling that something momentous was about to unfold, a sense of destiny pulling him inevitably forward.

He hid behind a bush and noticed the dragon descend near the house and roar as thunder erupted in the sky, a phenomenon he had not witnessed ever in his life. He saw as the dragon shrank and morphed its shape, slowly transforming from a gargantuan beast and then, much to Elian's surprise, into a gleaming woman. It was none other than Saraphina, who had reverted back into her human form. Elian was dumbfounded, and he began questioning himself,

"Is this why she said we cannot be together?"

As Elian watched Saraphina disappear into Iroh's dwelling, a whirlwind of emotions churned within him. Confusion mingled with a dawning realization, and a sense of betrayal gnawed at the edges of his consciousness. He couldn't fathom the depths of Saraphina's secret, nor could he comprehend the implications of her true nature.

Feeling a surge of determination, Elian emerged from his hiding place, his mind racing with unanswered questions. He approached the dwelling cautiously, his footsteps echoing in the stillness of the evening.

***

"Iroh, we need to talk," Saraphina entered the room with an air of aggression, her emotions fueled by a potent mix of anger and anxiety.

"What is it? Are you alright?" Iroh interrupted, concern evident in his voice as he noticed Saraphina's demeanor.

"What's not alright is that we're lying to him about all of this," Saraphina responded firmly, her tone unwavering.

"You do realize how strict the Council of Dragons is, right?" Iroh sighed, his expression reflecting a sense of resignation.

"I don't care about that; I just know I can't keep lying to him anymore. Why do these stupid rules even exist?" Saraphina's voice rose with frustration as she clenched her fists in defiance.

"They're there to maintain peace. Humans and Dragons cannot have connections between them. For millennia, humans hunted your kind for sport. You've been gifted with the power to bridge that gap, and it's not something to take lightly," Iroh explained, his tone somber.

Saraphina was momentarily speechless, her gaze shifting in disappointment between Iroh and the floor.

"I understand; I also fell in love with a dragon, and so did your parents..." Iroh's voice trailed off as he realized the gravity of his words, regret washing over him.

"You told me my parents left me when I was a child..." Saraphina's voice quivered with emotion as she confronted Iroh with the truth.

"There are some things I couldn't tell you for your own protection. Your parents had their reasons..." Iroh replied with a heavy sigh, the weight of his secrets burdening him.

"The only cruel thing right now is hiding the fact that both my parents have been dead for so many years!" Saraphina's anger flared, her frustration boiling over.

"Saraphina, calm down..." Iroh approached her cautiously, his hands raised in a gesture of peace.

Just as Saraphina was on the verge of losing her temper, the door creaked open with a loud sound, drawing everyone's attention. Standing in the doorway was Elian, who had been listening in on their conversation the entire time.

***

Elian's heart raced as he waited, each passing second feeling like an eternity. And then, with a creak, the door swung open, revealing Saraphina standing there. The expression on her face was a mix of surprise and disbelief.

"Elian?" she exclaimed, her voice betraying her astonishment.

"Is this why you told me you and I couldn't be together? Because of some council?" Elian blurted out; his frustration evident in his tone.

Saraphina, taken aback by his directness, hesitated before responding. "It's just... Iroh spoke to me about some things, and I can't shake off the weight of responsibility. I don't want anything to happen to you because of me."

Furrowing his brow, Elian searched her eyes for answers. "Iroh spoke to you? About us?"

Saraphina nodded, avoiding his gaze. "Yes, he did. He mentioned the complications of a relationship between a dragon shifter and a human. The Council of Dragons, their rules, Elian... it's complicated."

Elian paused, absorbing the gravity of their situation. "Saraphina, I don't care about rules or councils. I care about you. If there's a risk, let it be my choice to take. We can face whatever comes together."

Saraphina sighed, torn between her feelings for Elian and her desire to protect him. "Elian, it's not that simple. I care about you, too, but I can't ignore the potential consequences. I need time to figure things out."

Though disappointed, Elian respected her honesty. "Take the time you need, Saraphina. But know that my feelings haven't changed."

"No, you don't understand. I do have feelings for you as well. I don't want you to get hurt. Please," Saraphina pleaded tearfully.

"Sara, I can take care of myself. I have been on the outskirts for the longest time," Elian reassured her as he stepped closer.

"Elian, please…" Before she could finish, the distant roar of dragons echoed outside their house, interrupting their conversation.

"It's the council. You both need to go," Iroh stepped up as they heard the commotion outside. Saraphina's heart sank as she realized the severity of the situation. Without another word, she and Elian exchanged a knowing glance before hastily making their way outside, where the sky was ablaze with the presence of dragons.

Elian's jaw tensed as he scanned the horizon, his mind racing with the possibilities of what awaited them. "What do they want?" he muttered, more to himself than to anyone else.

Iroh's expression darkened as he stepped forward to join them. "They are here for inspections. It happens every month, and whenever they sense a sudden disturbance in the atmosphere, they use their senses to sniff out where the problem might be," he said gravely, his voice tinged with concern.

Saraphina's heart pounded against her ribs like a caged bird desperate for freedom. The news from Iroh had sent her mind spiraling into a whirlwind of fear and uncertainty, each breath feeling like a struggle against the weight of impending danger.

"In their eyes, you're a dragon," Iroh's words were like a chilling breeze, sending shivers down her spine. "They will perceive you as one and sense your emotions as one. When you were angry, it shifted the atmosphere and alerted them of imminent danger. All dragons are connected that way."

The dragons drew nearer, their massive forms casting ominous shadows over the trio. Saraphina's grip tightened on Elian's hand, seeking solace in the warmth of his touch amidst the encroaching darkness. Together, they stood in solidarity in a sea of uncertainty.

Iroh pressed a notebook into Saraphina's trembling hands. She flipped through its pages, her eyes scanning the words with a mixture of confusion and desperation. Each line seemed to hold a piece of the puzzle she had been searching for her entire life.

"This has all the answers you need," Iroh's voice was steady, but she could sense the undercurrent of urgency beneath his calm exterior. "Every question you've ever asked me, all the questions about your origin, your parents, everyone."

"What about you?" Saraphina's concern for Iroh was etched in every line of her face, every tremor in her voice.

"I will be fine, my child. Now go!" Iroh's words were firm, his gaze unwavering as he urged them on their way.

"Sara, we need to leave," Elian's urgency mirrored her own inner turmoil as he tugged gently on her hand, leading her toward safety.

Torn between the desire to stay and seek more answers and the need to flee from the impending danger, Saraphina hesitated. But Iroh's insistence left her no choice. With a heavy heart, she allowed Elian to guide her toward the backdoor, their escape route from the looming threat.

***

As Iroh approached the front door, his heart pounded with trepidation, knowing that the fate of Saraphina and Elian hung in the balance. Three dragons loomed before him, their presence casting a shadow over the once-peaceful scene.

"Where is the girl?" The lead dragon's voice echoed with authority, its eyes flashing with an intensity that sent shivers down Iroh's spine.

"What girl?" Iroh's voice rang out with a defiance that belied the fear coursing through his veins. "I see no girl here."

"Don't play coy with us," another dragon growled, its voice rumbling like thunder. "We sensed her in danger."

"I can assure you, there's no girl here," Iroh replied. His resolve remained unwavering despite the mounting pressure.

In the blink of an eye, the dragons unleashed their fury upon Iroh's home, flames licking at the walls and consuming everything in their path. Iroh watched helplessly as the place he had called home for so long was reduced to ash and rubble.

Once the dragons departed, leaving destruction in their wake, Iroh sank to his knees amidst the wreckage, his heart heavy with sorrow. Ellis, one of his beloved dragons, approached him, her eyes brimming with tears.

"Easy, girl. I'm okay," Iroh murmured, wrapping his arms around her massive form in a gesture of comfort. "Don't worry."

As he gazed up at the sky, now tinged with the orange glow of flames, Iroh offered a silent prayer for the safety of Saraphina and Elian. "Please be safe," he whispered, his words carried away by the wind.

Chapter 5: The Quest for Truth

Saraphina and Elian returned home later that night, having spent the day hidden in the cave. Clutching the notebook tightly to her chest, Saraphina felt a surge of emotions overwhelming her. She was restless, her mind plagued by thoughts of what might await them in the uncertain future.

Sensing her distress, Elian approached her. With a tenderness that spoke volumes, he took her in his arms, offering her solace in the midst of turmoil. Saraphina buried her face in his chest, seeking comfort in his embrace as tears streamed down her cheeks.

At that moment, words were unnecessary. The warmth of Elian's embrace and the steadiness of his presence were all she needed to find a fleeting sense of peace amidst the chaos. Together, they weathered the storm of emotions that threatened to consume them, finding strength in each other's arms.

Elian sighed, understanding the depth of Saraphina's frustration. "Iroh cares about you deeply, Saraphina. Maybe he thought he was protecting you by keeping certain things hidden," he suggested gently.

Saraphina shook her head. "But I'm not a child anymore, Elian. I can handle the truth, no matter how difficult it may be," she insisted, her resolve firm.

Elian reached out to her. His touch was gentle as he brushed a stray strand of hair from her face. "I know you can, Saraphina.

You're strong and capable, and I believe in you," he reassured her with unwavering resolve.

Elian's reassurance washed over Saraphina like a comforting wave, momentarily easing the turmoil within her. She leaned into his touch, finding solace in his steadfast presence amidst the chaos surrounding them.

"I know we will," Saraphina's voice wavered with emotion. "But what if we're not enough? What if Iroh needs us, and we're just sitting here, doing nothing?"

Elian's gaze softened, filled with empathy for her inner turmoil. "I understand your fears, Saraphina. But sometimes, the best thing we can do is trust those we care about and have faith that they'll find their way back to us."

Saraphina nodded, though her heart still felt heavy with worry. "I trust Iroh, but it's hard not knowing what's happening to him."

Elian squeezed her hand gently, offering silent support. "We'll keep a lookout, Saraphina. If there's any sign of trouble, we'll go to him. But for now, let's focus on what we can control."

With a deep breath, Saraphina nodded. "You're right, Elian. We'll wait, but we won't stay idle. We'll be ready." Determination flickered in her eyes.

Amidst the flickering glow of the fire and the weight of uncertainty hanging in the air, Saraphina and Elian found strength in each other, their bond growing stronger with each passing moment. Together, they would face whatever challenges lay ahead, united in their resolve to protect those they loved.

Saraphina looked up at him, her eyes reflecting a mixture of gratitude and apprehension. "But what if we can't, Elian? What if...?" Her voice trailed off, unable to voice the depths of her fears.

Elian cupped her face in his hands, his gaze unwavering as he met her eyes. "We'll face whatever comes our way, no matter how daunting it may seem. I'll protect you, Saraphina, I promise."

With Elian's reassurance, Saraphina felt a flicker of hope ignite within her heart, dispelling the shadows of doubt that threatened to consume her. Clutching onto his promise like a lifeline, she found the strength to face the challenges that lay ahead, knowing that with Elian by her side, they could overcome anything.

***

Elian had decided to take Saraphina back to the cave for hiding.

Deep within the cavern's dimly lit chambers, Saraphina and Elian's footsteps echoed softly against the walls as they ventured deeper into the darkness. The air was thick with anticipation, their hearts pounding in rhythm with the uncertainty that surrounded them.

As soon as they were deep enough in the cave enough to be undetected, Saraphina breathed fire on the nearby debris to light it up. This stunned Elian.

"You breathe fire as well?" Elian asked, shocked at the revelation.

"Yeah, heh. It is one of the traits of being a dragon. It makes one pretty much invincible," she continued. "Well, I mean not from any other dragon but from people, so..." Saraphina chuckled, scratching the back of her head.

As the flames danced around them, casting flickering shadows against the cave walls, Elian's gaze remained fixed on Saraphina, captivated by the mesmerizing glow of her fiery breath. Her embarrassed chuckle only added to the enchantment of the moment, filling the cavern with a warmth that transcended the physical fire.

"You're amazing," Elian repeated, his voice soft yet sincere as he spoke from the depths of his heart.

Saraphina's cheeks flushed with a deep crimson hue at his words, her eyes darting away momentarily before meeting his once more. "C'monnnn! I'm not even that pretty!" she protested, her laughter echoing through the cavern.

Elian shook his head, a fond smile playing on his lips. "It's not just your beauty, Saraphina. It's your strength, your courage, your fire... both literal and metaphorical," he confessed. The extent of his admiration was evident in his earnest gaze.

Saraphina's heart fluttered at his words, a warmth spreading through her chest despite the cool embrace of the cave. At that moment, surrounded by the echoes of their laughter and the gentle crackle of the flames, she felt a connection that went beyond words—a bond forged in the depths of adversity and strengthened by the fires of their shared journey.

With a shy smile, Saraphina reached out and took Elian's hand in hers, the warmth of their touch a comforting reminder of the strength they found in each other's presence.

Saraphina turned her attention to the diary Iroh had handed to her and began reading. Etched on the pages was extremely valuable information about Dragons, kinds Saraphina had never seen before.

Her eyes were opened wide in awe as she turned page after page. As she did, a note fell from the book, which read, "Draconia's Red Lotuses."

"Hmm?" Elian picked it up and showed it to Saraphina.

"I think this belongs to you," he continued.

"Draconia's Red Lotuses?" She muttered under her breath as she examined it before unfolding the large note, which revealed a bunch of notes noted down by Iroh on the Red Lotus Dragons.

According to the scribbles, the Red Lotus Dragons were of royalty and were considered the Faux Kings' of Draconia in the early Dragon War. Knights used to ride such dragons due to their violent nature and their ability to control fire. They were known for their striking crimson scales and fierce demeanor, often feared and revered in equal measure. Saraphina's breath caught in her throat as she delved deeper into the research, her mind reeling with the implications of her newfound knowledge.

"These Red Lotus Dragons... they were powerful beings," Saraphina murmured. Her voice was tinged with awe and reverence as she continued. "I never knew such dragons existed."

Elian looked carefully at the book and found a letter that was directed to Saraphina.

"What's this?" She looked at him, confused.

"It has your name on it. Iroh wrote it, I presume?" Elian added as he took the note book from her and went through it, leaving her to read the letter.

As she skimmed through the letter, Saraphina stumbled upon a tragic revelation: the once-majestic creatures had been driven to extinction centuries ago during the Great Dragon War. The pages spoke of a time when the Red Lotus Dragons reigned supreme, their fiery prowess unmatched by any other species. However, as the war ravaged Draconia, their numbers dwindled until they were no more.

Tears welled in Saraphina's eyes as she absorbed the weight of this devastating truth. The loss of such magnificent beings filled her with sorrow, and she couldn't help but feel a deep sense of mourning for her fallen kin.

As she flipped through the pages, another note caught her attention—a small parchment tucked away amidst the research. With trembling hands, she unfolded it and read the words inscribed upon it.

"To the last of the Red Lotus Dragons,

Saraphina, you carry within you the legacy of your kind. As the flames of our brethren flicker and fade into memory, you alone remain as the beacon of our heritage. Embrace your destiny, for you are the last guardian of the Red Lotus, a symbol of hope in a world plagued by darkness.

With courage and strength, may you rise and reclaim your rightful place among the stars.

— Iroh"

Saraphina's heart was overcome with emotion as she read the note again and again. The weight of her heritage bore down upon her, and she knew that her journey was not just one of discovery but that of redemption. With resolve burning in her chest, she vowed to honor the legacy of the Red Lotus Dragons and uncover the truth of their fate, no matter the cost.

"We have to find out more about them," Saraphina declared, her eyes sparkling with determination. "We have to uncover the truth behind the Red Lotus Dragons and how they went extinct without a trace."

"How will we do that?" Elian questioned as he stood there confused.

"Maybe if we read through the book, we might find out," Saraphina added as she took the book and began searching.

Elian nodded, "I'm with you on that."

Deep within the dimly lit cavern, Saraphina's eyes scanned the ancient pages of the notebook, her heart racing with anticipation. The writing, etched in the flowing script of ancient Draconian, seemed to dance before her eyes, each stroke a tantalizing clue to the mysteries of her heritage.

With a furrowed brow, Saraphina leaned in closer, her fingertips tracing the intricate patterns of the text as she attempted to decipher its meaning. The air was thick with the scent of damp earth and the faint crackle of the fire, casting eerie shadows that pranced across the walls of the cave.

Beside her, Elian stood to watch, his senses keenly attuned to the slightest hint of danger. His eyes swept the cavern's entrance, scanning the darkness for any signs of movement. With each passing moment, the weight of their precarious situation hung heavy in the air, a constant reminder of the dangers that lurked beyond the safety of their sanctuary.

As Saraphina delved deeper into the pages of the notebook, her frustration mounted with each cryptic passage. The language was archaic and unfamiliar, its meaning obscured by the passage of time. Yet she refused to be deterred, her determination unwavering in the face of adversity.

In the quiet expanse of the night, Elian stood watchful, his gaze unwavering as it traced the patterns of stars strewn across the sky. The darkness was broken only by the faint glow of celestial bodies, casting a gentle illumination over the landscape below. His senses were finely attuned to the subtlest of sounds, every rustle of leaves or whisper of wind sending a ripple of alertness through him. Years spent navigating the battlefield had sharpened his instincts to a keen edge.

Each passing moment seemed to add to the tension, thickening the air around him like a tangible cloak of unease. Within the confines of the cavern, an atmosphere of uncertainty hung heavily, suffusing the space with an almost palpable weight. Yet, amidst the encroaching shadows, a flicker of optimism persisted.

Saraphina, with her unyielding quest for truth, stood as a beacon amidst the gloom. Her determination mirrored Elian's own unwavering dedication to her safety, forging a bond that illuminated their path through the darkness. Together, they confronted the unknown with a courage born of conviction, prepared to unveil the mysteries concealed within the ancient pages of the enigmatic notebook.

"I found it!" Saraphina's voice pierced the stillness, breaking through the veil of silence with a note of triumph. Her smile, radiant against the backdrop of uncertainty, held the promise of discovery.

"Where is it? Where do we go?" Elian's curiosity interjected; his voice tinged with anticipation.

"Phoenix Island, the Land of Truth and Love," Saraphina's response carried a hint of excitement, a glimmer of anticipation dancing in her eyes.

"Wow, I was expecting something dark," Elian's disappointment was palpable, his expectations tempered by the weight of their journey.

"Oh, in that case, we'll have to traverse through the Woods of Dread," Saraphina's playful retort added a touch of mischief to the conversation, eliciting a nervous chuckle from Elian.

"Uh- yeah, no big deal! We can deal with it, yup!" Elian's bravado belied the flutter of apprehension in his heart, his resolve bolstered by Saraphina's infectious optimism.

As they concluded their search and readied themselves for the journey ahead, their packs laden with provisions and determination, they embarked on a quest shrouded in mystery. Their destination: to unravel the enigma of the Red Lotus Dragons' extinction and to uncover the truth behind Saraphina's extraordinary lineage as a Dragon Shifter. With each step forward, they ventured into the unknown, guided by the unwavering light of their shared purpose.

***

Saraphina and Elian began to carefully walk toward the top of the mountain in the middle of the night. It was a time when most dragons did not go out for patrols.

As they both approached the mountain top, Saraphina whispered the magic words,

"Oh Grande Draconia, accorde-moi la sagesse!"

Elian's eyes widened in wonder as Saraphina underwent a breathtaking metamorphosis before him. With a mesmerizing grace, her form shifted and contorted, gradually morphing into that of a majestic dragon. He watched in awe as her once-human features were replaced by scales of iridescent hues, shimmering in the faint starlight. Wings, vast and splendid, unfurled from her back, casting shadows that danced across the cavern walls.

"Quick question, do the clothes transform as well, or do they just, you know...?" Elian's inquiry broke the spell of astonishment. His voice was tinged with a mix of curiosity and amusement.

Saraphina chuckled, the sound echoing softly. "Hehe, hop on!" she beckoned, extending a clawed hand toward him. Elian hesitated for just a moment before accepting her offer, settling himself upon her neck with a mixture of trepidation and exhilaration.

With a powerful thrust of her wings, Saraphina propelled them both into the air, leaving the confines of the cavern far below. The rush of wind whipped against Elian's face as they ascended higher and higher, the ground shrinking into insignificance beneath them. The sensation of flight was unlike anything he had ever experienced, a heady mixture of freedom and exhilaration.

Together, they soared through the night sky, their journey illuminated by the gentle glow of the moon and stars above. As they navigated the vast expanse of the heavens, Elian couldn't help but marvel at the sheer magnificence of their surroundings. With Saraphina as his guide, he felt as though he had been granted access to a world beyond his wildest dreams.

Chapter 6: The Power of Love

High above the sprawling landscape of Draconia, Elian and Saraphina soared through the azure sky, her wings slicing effortlessly through the air. The wind whispered through their scales, carrying with it the scent of pine and wildflowers as they ventured to new horizons.

With each passing moment, their bond grew stronger. They visited hidden valleys and ancient ruins, their laughter echoing across the vast expanse of the land as they explored the wonders of Draconia.

As they flew, Elian and Saraphina felt the warmth of each other's presence, a comforting reminder of the deep connection that blossomed between them. In the quiet moments between their adventures, they shared whispered conversations and stolen glances, their hearts overflowing with affection.

For two days, Elian and Saraphina traversed the breathtaking landscapes of Draconia, their wings carrying them across towering mountains, lush forests, and shimmering lakes. They delved deeper into the heart of the land, exploring its hidden wonders and untamed beauty.

As they journeyed together, their love blossomed like a delicate flower unfurling its petals under the warmth of the sun. They shared whispered words and tender touches, their hearts entwined with each passing moment. In the embrace of the open sky, they reveled in the simple joy of being together, their laughter echoing across the vast expanse of the heavens.

With each discovery they made, their bond grew stronger, like the roots of an ancient tree sinking ever deeper into the rich soil. They marveled at the wonders of nature around them, their spirits lifted by the sheer magnificence of the world they inhabited. In each other's arms, they found solace and strength. Together, they were ready to face whatever challenges lay ahead, knowing that they could overcome anything as one.

In the heart of Draconia lay Phoenix Island, a mystical enclave whispered about in tales of love and destiny. As Elian and Saraphina approached its shores, the air seemed to hum with otherworldly energy tinged with the promise of profound connection and enduring bonds.

Phoenix Island's allure lay not only in its picturesque beauty but also in the ancient legends that enshrouded it. According to lore passed down through generations, this island held the power to bind two souls together in an unbreakable union—a place where love transcended the confines of time and space.

Stepping onto the pristine sands of Phoenix Island, Elian and Saraphina felt a sense of admiration wash over them. The landscape unfolded before them like a vibrant canvas, whispering the symphony of nature's chorus.

The island was adorned with lush, lively flora, and their blossoms painted the landscape with a riot of colors. The air was perfumed with the sweet scent of flowers, carrying with it a sense of serenity and tranquility.

Elian and Saraphina wandered hand in hand through the winding paths of the island, their footsteps soft against the verdant earth. Around them, the gentle rustle of leaves and the melodious trill of birdsong filled the air, creating a symphony of nature's harmony.

They came upon a secluded grove, nestled beneath the shade of towering trees, where a crystal-clear spring bubbled forth from the earth. The water sparkled in the dappled sunlight, casting shimmering reflections upon the surrounding foliage.

On Phoenix Island, legends whispered of a sacred ritual performed by lovers from time immemorial — a ritual that bound their hearts together for eternity. Elian and Saraphina felt the weight of history and tradition in the air, mingling with the heady fragrance of the flowers.

As they ventured further inland, they encountered a maze of verdant pathways, each leading deeper into the heart of the island's enchantment. The air was thick with the heady fragrance of blooming flowers, their petals glistening with dewdrops as if kissed by the morning sun.

As Elian and Saraphina meandered through the bustling markets of Draconia, they were met with whispers of an extraordinary event—the Blossom Festival. The locals spoke of it in hushed tones, their eyes alight with reverence for the celestial spectacle that graced the skies once every century.

Intrigued by the tales they heard, Elian and Saraphina eagerly inquired further, their curiosity piqued by the promise of witnessing such a rare and wondrous phenomenon. They learned that the Blossom Festival was a breathtaking display of nature's majesty. The night sky would be illuminated by a cascade of ethereal blossoms, painting the heavens in a kaleidoscope of colors.

Determined to partake in this once-in-a-lifetime event, Elian and Saraphina set about making preparations. They sought out local artisans and merchants, procuring vibrant garments adorned with intricate designs reminiscent of the blooming flowers that would grace the skies above. Each detail was carefully chosen, and each accessory was selected with the utmost care as they sought to honor the spirit of the festival in their attire.

As the day of the festival drew near, Elian and Saraphina's excitement bubbled over, their hearts dancing with anticipation. They joined the throngs of revelers who had gathered from far and wide, their spirits buoyed by the collective energy of the crowd.

As twilight descended and the first stars began to twinkle overhead, Elian and Saraphina stood hand in hand, their eyes fixed on the horizon. They waited with bated breath, eager to bear witness to the celestial spectacle that awaited them—the Blossom Festival, a celebration of love and unity that would linger in their memories for eternity.

Amidst the enchanting ambiance of the Blossom Festival, Elian's heart swelled with emotion. He turned to Saraphina; his gaze soft yet filled with an intensity that mirrored the depth of his feelings.

"Saraphina, since the moment I met you, I knew there was something special about you. Your kindness, your strength, your unwavering spirit—it's like your heart is made of pure gold, radiating warmth and light wherever you go."

Saraphina's eyes shimmered with emotion as she listened to his heartfelt words, her own heart skipping a beat at the sincerity in his voice. In that moment, surrounded by the beauty of the Blossom Festival, she felt a profound connection to Elian, a bond that transcended time and space.

"Elian," she replied, her voice barely above a whisper, "You've brought so much joy and light into my life. I'm grateful every day that our paths crossed." With a trembling hand, she reached up to gently caress his cheek, her touch tender and full of unspoken affection.

Their eyes met in the soft glow of the moonlight, and a silent exchange of emotions passed between them. And then, as if drawn together by an invisible force, their lips met in a sweet and tender kiss—a moment of pure magic amidst the splendor of the Blossom Festival.

Time seemed to stand still as they lingered in each other's embrace, their hearts beating as one. In that fleeting moment, surrounded by the beauty of nature's spectacle and the warmth of their love, Elian and Saraphina knew that they had found something truly extraordinary—a love that would endure for all eternity.

As Elian and Saraphina basked in the serene atmosphere of Phoenix Island, a deafening roar echoed across the island as the Council of Dragons descended upon them, their imposing presence casting a shadow over the once-peaceful landscape.

"I have you surrounded, Dragon Shifter," the dragon roared. "There is no need for you to run, surrender yourself!"

Elian's grip tightened instinctively around Saraphina's hand as they watched in horror as the dragons began to wreak havoc, their powerful wings beating against the sky like thunderous drums. Flames erupted from their mouths, painting the night sky with streaks of fiery red as they unleashed their fury upon the unsuspecting island.

Panic rippled through the crowd as people fled in all directions, seeking refuge from the onslaught of destruction. Saraphina's heart raced with fear as she clung to Elian, her eyes wide with disbelief at the sudden turn of events.

"We have to get out of here!" Elian shouted over the roar of the dragons; his voice filled with urgency as he pulled Saraphina toward the safety of the forest. Saraphina's resolve hardened as she felt the weight of Elian's hand slip from hers. In an instant, her form began to shimmer and contort, her human guise melting away to reveal the true essence of her being—a majestic dragon, her scales gleaming in the moonlight as she unleashed her fury upon the invaders.

With a deafening roar, Saraphina lunged into battle, her wings beating against the air with thunderous force as she clashed with the dragons from the Council. Flames erupted from her jaws, lighting up the night sky as she fought tooth and claw to defend the island and its people.

But even as she fought with all her strength, Saraphina found herself outnumbered and overpowered by the relentless assault of her adversaries. The dragons from the Council pressed their advantage, their sheer size and ferocity overwhelming her defenses as they battered her with a barrage of blows.

With each strike, Saraphina felt the force of the impact reverberate through her body, her strength waning with every passing moment. She gritted her teeth against the pain, refusing to yield even as the ground trembled beneath her and her vision blurred with exhaustion.

Despite her valiant efforts, Saraphina could feel herself faltering, her movements growing sluggish as the dragons from the Council closed in for the final blow. With a mighty roar, they descended upon her. Their combined might crashed down upon her in a torrent of fury and destruction.

As the darkness closed in around her, Saraphina fought to hold on, her heart filled with determination even in the face of defeat. But as the weight of the dragons bore down upon her, she knew that this battle would not end in victory—and that the fate of Phoenix Island hung in the balance.

As the menacing dragon loomed closer, its fiery breath searing the air around them, Elian stepped protectively in front of Saraphina, his stance resolute as he faced down their formidable foe. "I won't let you harm her," he declared, his voice unwavering despite the tremble in his heart.

With a thunderous roar, the dragon charged up its flames, a blaze of inferno gathering in its gaping maw as it prepared to unleash its deadly assault upon them. But just as the dragon released its fiery torrent, a brilliant light enveloped Saraphina, her form glowing with an otherworldly radiance.

In that moment, she became a beacon of blazing energy, her very essence infused with the power of the dragons. With a defiant roar of her own, Saraphina unleashed her own torrent of flames, a searing inferno that engulfed the dragon's wings in a blaze of white-hot fire.

The dragon shrieked in agony as its wings burned, the flames licking hungrily at its scales as it recoiled in pain. Caught off guard by Saraphina's sudden display of power, the dragon faltered, its attack disrupted as it struggled to regain its footing amidst the chaos.

Elian watched in awe as Saraphina unleashed her fiery wrath upon their assailant, his heart swelling with pride and admiration for the courageous dragon by his side. Together, they stood united against the forces of darkness, their bond forged in the heat of battle as they faced their greatest trial yet.

Saraphina transformed back into a human and looked at Elian as she nodded and held his hand. Together, they sprinted through the chaos, dodging flames and debris as they escaped.

However, even as they ran, the sound of the fiery mess in their ears constantly reminded them of the danger that lurked just beyond the trees. With each passing moment, the situation grew direr, their hopes of escape dwindling with every step.

As they disappeared into the safety of the forest, a sense of unease settled over them, their hearts heavy with the knowledge that the Council of Dragons would stop at nothing to achieve their sinister goals. With them seeking refuge amidst the trees, Elian and Saraphina knew that their journey was far from over and that the path ahead would be fraught with danger and uncertainty.

As they found a moment of respite in the shelter of the forest, Saraphina's shoulders slumped with the weight of sorrow, her eyes reflecting the turmoil within her soul. Elian approached her gently, sensing her distress, and reached out to grasp her hand in his.

"Are you okay?" Elian asked as he saw tears well up in her eyes.

"I never imagined it would come to this. The Council's attack, the destruction... I feel responsible for all of it," Saraphina mourned as she sighed and looked down.

"You're not alone in this," he replied, his tone filled with unwavering support. "We'll face this together every step of the way. You don't have to carry the weight of the world on your shoulders."

"Your heart is pure. You never meant to cause all of this destruction. I know for a fact that instead, you helped everyone on this island," he added.

Saraphina nodded as she sniffled. "Will you hold me?" She inquired as she looked at him.

He instantly enveloped her in his arms and began to caress her hair, swaying her softly. In that moment, they found solace in each other's presence as their bond was forged anew in the crucible of danger.

Chapter 7: Trials and Tribulations

Embraced by the comforting sanctuary of the forest, Saraphina and Elian found themselves at a crossroads. Their path forward was shrouded in uncertainty yet illuminated by the flickering flame of hope. As they sat together beneath the verdant canopy of trees, the urgency of their situation weighed heavily upon them, each moment pregnant with the potential for danger.

Saraphina leaned against a gnarled tree trunk, her eyes reflecting the dim light filtering through the dense foliage above. Beside her, Elian's gaze was resolute, his jaw set with determination as he contemplated their next move.

"We can't stay here for long," Elian murmured, breaking the heavy silence that enveloped them. "The council's forces will be scouring every inch of this forest in search of us."

Saraphina nodded in agreement, a knot of apprehension tightening in her chest. "But where do we go from here?" she wondered aloud; her voice tinged with uncertainty.

Elian considered her question for a moment before responding. "We need to keep moving," he said firmly. "We can't risk staying in one place for too long. We'll have to travel on foot, using the cover of the forest to shield us from prying eyes."

Saraphina's heart sank at the prospect of their perilous journey ahead, but she knew there was no other choice. With a determined nod, she rose to her feet, her resolve steeling her against the encroaching darkness.

"We'll make it through this, Saraphina," Elian assured her, his voice a beacon of reassurance in the gloom. "Together, we'll find our way to safety."

With renewed determination, Saraphina and Elian set out into the forest, their footsteps echoing softly against the forest floor as they embarked on their journey into the unknown. Hand in hand, they prepared to face the challenges that lay ahead; their bond forged stronger with each step they took toward an uncertain future.

As Saraphina and Elian ventured deeper into the forest, they found themselves surrounded by an ethereal beauty that seemed to shimmer with the whispers of ancient magic. The air was alive with the soft hum of unseen creatures, and the gentle rustle of leaves overhead filled them with a sense of wonder.

Suddenly, emerging from the shadows of the forest, Saraphina spotted a majestic creature with a spiraling horn, its pure white coat gleaming in the soft light filtering through the canopy above. It was a unicorn, its eyes filled with a wisdom that seemed to transcend time itself.

"Tobias, is that you?" Saraphina whispered in awe, recognizing the unicorn from the stories she had heard as a child. The unicorn regarded her with a gentle gaze, its presence radiating a sense of serenity that washed over them like a soothing balm.

Elian's eyes widened in wonder as he beheld the mythical creature before them. "Is that... a unicorn? You know him?" he breathed; his voice filled with disbelief.

Saraphina nodded, her heart brimming with reverence for the magical being before them. "Yes. Tobias used to visit our home, but then he had to migrate with the rest of his family," she replied, her voice barely above a whisper.

Approaching the unicorn with cautious reverence, Saraphina reached out a hand, her fingertips brushing against Tobias's velvety coat. To her surprise, the unicorn nuzzled her hand affectionately, its gentle eyes filled with a silent understanding.

"We're in need of a sanctuary," Saraphina explained, her voice filled with urgency. "Can you help us?"

In response, Tobias nodded solemnly as if sensing the gravity of their situation. With a graceful motion, the unicorn gestured for them to follow. Its steps were sure and steady as it led them deeper into the heart of the forest.

As they followed Tobias, Saraphina, and Elian felt a sense of peace wash over them, their worries momentarily forgotten in the presence of such a magical being. Finally, after what seemed like an eternity, they arrived at a secluded glade bathed in golden sunlight.

"This will be our sanctuary," Saraphina whispered, her voice filled with gratitude as she surveyed their surroundings. "Here, we can rest and gather our strength before continuing our journey."

With a heartfelt nod of thanks to Tobias, Saraphina, and Elian settled into the sanctuary, their hearts filled with hope for the trials that lay ahead. In the tranquil embrace of the forest, surrounded by the whispers of ancient magic, they found solace in the knowledge that they were not alone on their quest for safety and answers.

***

As they luxuriated in the soothing waters of a nearby spring, Saraphina and Elian felt the weariness of their journey melt away, replaced by a sense of renewal and rejuvenation. The gentle caress of the water against their skin seemed to wash away the dust and grime of their travels, leaving them feeling refreshed and invigorated.

After they had bathed and cleaned themselves, Saraphina and Elian found a quiet spot within the sanctuary, surrounded by the gentle rustle of leaves and the distant chirping of birds. Sitting side by side, they allowed themselves a moment of respite, the weight of their worries momentarily lifted in the tranquil embrace of their surroundings.

With a heavy sigh, Saraphina turned to Elian, her eyes filled with a mixture of sorrow and apprehension. "I can't shake this feeling of dread, Elian," she confessed, her voice barely above a whisper. "The events of today... they've shaken me to my core."

Elian reached out a comforting hand, his touch a reassuring presence against her trembling shoulder. "I know, Saraphina," he murmured softly. "But we can't let fear consume us. We have to stay strong for each other."

Saraphina nodded, her heart heavy with the weight of their shared burden. "I just... I can't help but worry about what lies ahead," she admitted. Her voice was trembling with emotion. "What if we can't outrun the Council? What if they catch up to us?"

Elian squeezed her hand gently, his eyes filled with determination. "We'll face whatever comes together, Saraphina," he vowed, his voice unwavering in its conviction. "We've come this far, and we won't let anything stand in our way."

"I don't know if I can keep you safe. I feel like I'm dragging you into danger, and I can't bear the thought of anything happening to you because of me."

Elian's brow furrowed in concern as he reached out to gently brush a stray lock of hair from Saraphina's face. "Saraphina, I'm here because I want to be. I made that choice willingly, knowing the risks. You're not dragging me into anything—I'm here because I care about you, and I'll do whatever it takes to keep you safe."

Tears welled in Saraphina's eyes as she listened to Elian's heartfelt words, her heart aching with the weight of his unwavering devotion. "But what if something happens to you because of me?" she whispered, her voice trembling with fear.

Elian took her hands in his, his touch a comforting anchor amidst the storm of her emotions. "Saraphina, I would rather face any danger by your side than live a life without you," he said, his voice filled with quiet determination. "We'll face whatever comes our way together."

Despite Elian's reassurances, Saraphina couldn't shake the feeling of dread that lingered in the depths of her heart. As the weight of her fears threatened to overwhelm her, she knew that she had to protect him, even if it meant pushing him away.

"Elian," she said, her voice trembling with emotion, "I think...
I think you should leave. It's for your own good. I can't risk your
safety any longer."

Elian's eyes widened in shock at her words, his heart aching
with the pain of her rejection. "Saraphina, no," he protested, his
voice filled with anguish. "I won't leave you, not now, not ever.
We'll face this together, I promise."

But Saraphina's resolve remained firm, her gaze filled with a
mixture of sorrow and determination. "Please, Elian," she
pleaded, her voice barely above a whisper. "For your own sake,
go."

As Elian rose silently and left, the weight of his departure hung
heavy in the air, casting a shadow over the sanctuary that had
once been a refuge from their troubles. Saraphina watched him
go, her heart heavy with the burden of her decision, her own
insecurities gnawing at the edges of her mind.

Alone now, Saraphina felt the void in her heart grow with each
passing moment, a tangible ache that echoed the emptiness she
felt inside. She had pushed Elian away out of fear, out of a
desperate need to protect him from the dangers that loomed on
the horizon, but now she couldn't shake the feeling that she had
made a terrible mistake.

As she sat in the quiet sanctuary, the soft glow of moonlight
filtering through the trees overhead, Saraphina found herself
grappling with the overwhelming weight of her own insecurities.
She had allowed her fears to dictate her actions, to drive a wedge
between her and the one person who had stood by her side
through thick and thin.

Tears welled in Saraphina's eyes as she realized the depth of her mistake, the magnitude of the distance she had placed between herself and Elian. She longed to reach out to him, to beg for his forgiveness. But she knew deep down that she had to confront her own fears before she could ever hope to mend what had been broken between them.

With a heavy heart, Saraphina curled up in the sanctuary, the soft rustle of leaves outside a haunting reminder of the rift that now lay between her and Elian. In the silence of the night, she whispered a silent prayer, a plea for strength and guidance as she faced the daunting journey ahead alone.

As Saraphina lay curled up in the sanctuary, her mind wandered to thoughts of Iroh, the father figure who had always been there for her, offering guidance and support when she needed it most. The memory of his comforting presence filled her with a profound sense of longing, a deep ache for the warmth of his embrace and the reassurance of his words.

In the quiet solitude of the sanctuary, surrounded by the gentle rustle of leaves and the soft glow of moonlight filtering through the trees, Saraphina felt a wave of loneliness wash over her, threatening to engulf her in its suffocating embrace. The weight of her solitude pressed down on her like a heavy stone, crushing her spirit beneath its relentless burden.

Unable to contain her emotions any longer, Saraphina buried her face in her hands and let out a heart-wrenching sob. The sound echoed through the stillness of the night like a mournful cry for help. Tears streamed down her cheeks, hot and bitter against her skin, as she grappled with the overwhelming sense of fear and uncertainty that consumed her from within.

In that moment of vulnerability, Saraphina felt more alone than ever before, the vast expanse of the forest stretching out around her like an endless void of darkness and despair. She longed for Iroh's comforting presence, for the reassuring sound of his voice and the strength of his embrace, but she knew that he was far beyond her reach now, lost to her in a world consumed by chaos and turmoil.

As her tears continued to fall, mingling with the soft earth beneath her and the gentle whispers of the night, Saraphina found solace in the knowledge that she was not truly alone. Though Iroh might not be by her side, his love and guidance were always with her, a beacon of hope in the darkness that surrounded her.

With a deep, shuddering breath, Saraphina closed her eyes and surrendered herself to the embrace of sleep. She knew that when she awoke, she would face whatever challenges lay ahead with courage and determination, for Iroh would be with her every step of the way in spirit.

***

As Saraphina slowly stirred from her slumber, she was enveloped in the warmth of Elian's embrace, his strong arms wrapped protectively around her. The events of the previous night flooded back to her in a rush of emotions, and she felt a swell of gratitude wash over her at the sight of him lying there beside her. His features seemed to have softened in the gentle light of dawn.

Silent tears welled up in Saraphina's eyes as she gazed upon Elian's sleeping form, overwhelmed by the depth of emotion stirring within her. At that moment, she felt a profound sense of connection to him, a bond that transcended words and spoke directly to her soul.

Despite the weight of her sorrow and the uncertainty that still hung heavy in the air, Saraphina found solace in the knowledge that she was not alone. With Elian by her side, she felt a glimmer of hope flicker to life within her heart, a beacon of light amidst the darkness that threatened to consume her.

Taking a deep, steadying breath, Saraphina reached out to gently brush a stray lock of hair from Elian's forehead, her touch light and tender against his skin. She lingered there for a moment, savoring the warmth of his presence and the comfort of his embrace, before finally allowing herself to relax into the peaceful stillness of the morning.

As the first rays of sunlight filtered through the shelter above, casting a golden glow upon their secluded sanctuary, Saraphina closed her eyes and let herself be consumed by the quiet beauty of the moment.

As Saraphina drifted into a daydream, her thoughts swirling with worries and uncertainties, she felt a shift in the air as Elian stirred beside her. Hastily, she averted her gaze, a flicker of embarrassment coloring her cheeks as she pretended to be absorbed in the surroundings of their sanctuary.

Elian's gentle touch roused Saraphina from her reverie, and she blinked in surprise, still avoiding his gaze. As she felt the soft press of his lips against hers, a rush of warmth flooded her heart, dispelling the lingering shadows of her worries.

Slowly, tentatively, Saraphina turned to meet Elian's eyes, finding comfort and reassurance in the tender affection reflected in his gaze. His presence was a beacon of light in the darkness, offering solace and strength in the face of her fears.

"Everything will be alright, Saraphina," Elian murmured softly, his voice a soothing melody that eased the turmoil in her soul. Despite her lingering doubts, his words filled her with a sense of hope and determination.

Unable to resist any longer, Saraphina leaned into his embrace, seeking refuge in the warmth of his arms. With Elian by her side, she felt a renewed sense of courage, ready to face whatever challenges lay ahead.

As they lingered together in the quiet embrace of the morning, Saraphina allowed herself to believe, if only for a moment, that perhaps everything truly would be alright. In Elian's unwavering presence, she found the strength to confront whatever the future held.

Chapter 8: Betrayal and Redemption

The first rays of dawn filtered through the foliage, casting a golden hue upon the tranquil sanctuary where Saraphina and Elian had found solace for the night. As they stirred from their slumber, they exchanged a silent glance filled with unspoken gratitude for the refuge provided by Tobias, the gentle Unicorn who had guided them to safety.

With a soft smile, Saraphina reached out to stroke Tobias' mane, silently thanking him for his kindness and guidance. The Unicorn nuzzled her affectionately in return, his eyes conveying understanding and reassurance.

"Thank you, Tobias," Elian said, his voice filled with sincerity as he patted the Unicorn's flank. "We wouldn't have made it through the night without you."

As they bid farewell to their friend, Saraphina and Elian set out once more, their footsteps echoing softly against the forest floor. With determination in their hearts and a sense of purpose guiding their steps, they made their way toward the towering mountains looming in the distance.

As Saraphina unfolded the map, her eyes traced the intricate lines and symbols that marked their journey ahead. Among the various destinations sprawled across the parchment, one stood out to her—the Temple of the Dragons.

"It's not far from here," she murmured, her voice tinged with a mix of determination and trepidation.

Elian nodded in agreement, casting a cautious glance at the looming mountains in the distance. "But it would be unwise to approach by air. The Council's dragons could easily spot us."

With a resigned sigh, Saraphina folded the map once more, tucking it safely into her satchel. "Then we'll have to travel on foot," she conceded, though the prospect of a long and arduous journey ahead weighed heavily on her mind.

As they set out on their journey, the landscape offered them a mix of history and legend. Ancient temples and forgotten ruins dotted their path, each bearing witness to the rich Draconian heritage.

Saraphina and Elian paused at each site, marveling at the intricacy of the carvings and the stories etched into the stone. With each step, they felt a deeper connection to the land and its ancient inhabitants, their footsteps echoing through the corridors of time.

Despite the dangers that lurked in the shadows, they pressed onward, their resolve unwavering in the face of adversity. They knew that their journey held the key to unlocking the mysteries of Saraphina's past and securing their future together.

As the sun dipped below the horizon, casting the sky in a fiery hue, Saraphina and Elian found themselves by the tranquil waters of a secluded lake. They had set up camp for the night, the crackling wood fire casting a warm glow upon their faces as they sat side by side, their fingers entwined in silent solidarity.

Saraphina's gaze drifted across the rippling surface of the lake; her thoughts weighed down by the burden of their journey and the uncertainty that lay ahead. She couldn't shake the feeling of guilt that gnawed at her heart for her earlier words, words spoken in haste and borne of fear.

Elian sensed her inner turmoil and gently turned to face her; his eyes soft with understanding. "Hey," he murmured, his voice a soothing balm to her troubled soul.

"I know you're scared, Saraphina. But you don't have to face this alone. I'm here for you, no matter what."

His words washed over her like a gentle tide, dispelling the shadows of doubt that clouded her mind. Saraphina felt a swell of gratitude wash over her, mingled with a deep-seated sense of relief. She leaned into Elian's embrace, seeking solace in the warmth of his presence.

With a heavy heart, she met his gaze, her eyes brimming with unspoken apology. "I'm sorry for what I said earlier," she murmered, her voice barely above a whisper. "I didn't mean to push you away."

Elian reached out, gently cupping her cheek with his hand. "It's okay, Saraphina," he reassured her, his touch a gentle caress against her skin. "We all have our moments of fear and doubt. But we're in this together, remember?"

A soft smile tugged at the corners of Saraphina's lips as she leaned in, closing the distance between them. Their lips met in a tender kiss, a silent promise of unity and unwavering devotion. In that moment, all their worries and fears melted away, leaving only the warmth of their love to light the path forward.

As the night unfolded around them, they shared intimate moments by the flickering firelight, their hearts entwined in a bond that transcended the trials of their journey. Together, they faced the darkness of the unknown, drawing strength from the unwavering certainty of their love.

***

As Saraphina and Elian approached the Temple of the Dragons, their footsteps slowed in awe of the majestic structure that loomed before them. The temple rose from the earth like a towering sentinel, its grandeur casting a spell of reverence upon all who beheld it.

Saraphina's breath caught in her throat as she gazed upon the temple's exterior, her eyes tracing the intricate carvings that adorned its walls. The air hummed with palpable energy as if the very stones themselves held ancient secrets waiting to be unlocked.

With a sense of anticipation tingling in her veins, Saraphina hurried forward, her steps quickening as she crossed the threshold into the temple's hallowed halls. As she entered, her eyes widened in wonder at the sight that greeted her.

The interior of the temple was a breathtaking display of beauty and grandeur. Sunlight streamed through stained glass windows, casting vibrant hues of light upon the polished marble floors. Ornate tapestries adorned the walls, depicting scenes from Draconian mythology in vivid detail.

Saraphina was enraptured by the sheer magnificence of it all, her heart swelling with a sense of reverence and awe. She felt as though she had stepped into another world, a realm where the boundaries between the mortal and the divine blurred and faded away.

Elian stood beside her; his own gaze filled with wonder as he took in the splendor of the temple. Together, they explored its halls, their footsteps echoing against the stone walls as they marveled at the beauty that surrounded them.

At that moment, amidst the grandeur of the Temple of the Dragons, Saraphina felt a sense of peace wash over her. As Saraphina ventured further into the depths of the temple, she discovered chamber after chamber filled with ancient scrolls and tomes, their pages filled with the wisdom and knowledge of ages passed. The air was thick with the scent of parchment and dust, and the soft glow of flickering torches illuminated the vast expanse of the library.

Her eyes widened in amazement as she realized the true purpose of the temple—it served as a repository of knowledge, a sacred archive containing the collective wisdom of generations of dragons.

Saraphina's heart raced with excitement as she ran her fingers over the weathered spines of the books, her mind buzzing with the possibilities that lay within their pages. Here, she would find answers to the questions that had plagued her for so long, insights into her own heritage and the mysteries of the dragon world.

As she delved deeper into the library's depths, she uncovered scrolls detailing the histories of ancient dragon clans, their triumphs, and tragedies etched into the annals of time. She marveled at intricate maps depicting the vast expanse of Draconia, dotted with landmarks shrouded in myth and legend.

With each discovery, Saraphina's thirst for knowledge grew, fueled by the boundless treasures that lay hidden within the temple's walls.

As Saraphina delved deeper into the ancient tome, her eyes widened in astonishment as she stumbled upon a section detailing the lives of her parents. Their names leaped off the page, written in an elegant script that spoke of a time long past but not forgotten. With bated breath, she read on, her heart pounding with anticipation as she uncovered the truth of her lineage.

While Iroh's notes had already revealed that she came from the line of Red Lotus Dragons, what Saraphina didn't know was that she was hailed as the strongest of the Red Lotus Dragons, a title bestowed upon her for her unique abilities and unwavering determination.

She was not just any dragon; she was the culmination of centuries of evolution, the pinnacle of her kind.

But it was the revelation of her true power that truly took her breath away. She read with awe as the words described her ability to transform willingly into a human—a feat unheard of among her kind for millennia. It was a gift bestowed upon her by destiny, a testament to her innate strength and resilience.

And as if that weren't enough, she learned of another extraordinary ability that set her apart from all others. When in contact with deep emotions, Saraphina had the power to summon a godly flame armor, a formidable force that could turn the tide of any battle. It was a power that she had only begun to understand, but one that filled her with a sense of awe and reverence.

As she absorbed the magnitude of her own abilities, Saraphina felt a surge of pride and determination coursing through her veins. Saraphina was a beacon of hope, a symbol of resilience in the face of adversity. And as she closed the book, her heart brimming with newfound confidence, she knew that she was destined for greatness.

As Saraphina shared the astounding revelations with Elian, his eyes mirrored her astonishment. Together, they marveled at the incredible truth laid bare before them, their hearts swelling with a newfound sense of purpose and wonder.

Their moment of shared awe was abruptly interrupted by the unexpected appearance of a familiar figure. It was Iroh. His presence was both a comfort and a cause for concern. Saraphina's heart skipped a beat at the sight of him, a rush of conflicting emotions washing over her.

However, her joy quickly turned to apprehension as Iroh's words echoed in the chamber. His gaze hardened as he addressed Saraphina, his tone firm and resolute.

"Saraphina, my child," he began, his voice tinged with sadness and regret, "you must leave Elian. It's not safe for you to be with him any longer."

"I won't leave, Iroh," she asserted, her voice trembling with a mix of determination and fear. "I'm done running."

As she stood her ground, a sudden gust of wind swept through the temple, heralding the arrival of Eris, Iroh's dragon. With a deafening roar, Eris swooped down, her massive form pinning Saraphina and Elian to the ground with irresistible force.

Caught off guard by the sudden assault, Saraphina and Elian struggled against Eris' hold, their efforts in vain against the dragon's formidable strength. Within moments, the chamber was filled with the presence of the Council of Dragons, their imposing figures casting a shadow over the room.

Saraphina and Elian were subdued by the council's power, their struggles futile against the overwhelming might arrayed against them. As they were held captive, Iroh stood nearby, his head bowed in shame and regret.

His heart felt heavy with the consequences of his actions. Despite his conflicted feelings, Iroh knew that he had chosen his path, and now, he was forced to face the consequences.

Saraphina's gaze bore into Iroh's, her eyes filled with a mix of anger, confusion, and hurt. "Why, Iroh?" she demanded, her voice trembling with emotion. "Why would you betray us like this?"

Iroh remained silent, his expression unreadable as he struggled to find the words to respond. For a moment, the only sound in the chamber was the echoing beat of their hearts, the weight of unspoken truths pressing down upon them.

Finally, Iroh spoke in a whisper. "I thought I was protecting you," he admitted, his words laced with regret. "But I see now that I only brought you more pain."

Saraphina's eyes softened, her anger giving way to sorrow as she realized the depth of Iroh's guilt. "Iroh, we trusted you," she murmured, her voice filled with a sense of betrayal. "Why didn't you trust us?"

Iroh lowered his head, unable to meet Saraphina's gaze. "I was afraid," he confessed, his voice barely audible. "Afraid of what the council would do if they found out about you."

Saraphina's heart ached at Iroh's admission, her own pain mirrored in his words. Despite everything, she couldn't help but feel a pang of sympathy for the man who had been like a father to her.

But even as she struggled to reconcile her conflicting emotions, Saraphina knew that their trust had been shattered, irreparably broken by Iroh's betrayal. As she stood there, grappling with the aftermath of his actions, she couldn't help but wonder if their bond would ever be the same again.

Chapter 9: A New Beginning

As Saraphina's consciousness gradually emerged from the haze of sleep, she found herself in a dimly lit dungeon, the cold stone walls closing in around her. The air was thick with musk and dampness, sending a chill down her spine. Confusion clouded her mind as she tried to piece together how she had ended up in this desolate place.

The sound of tapping drew her attention, and she turned her gaze toward the source. Standing outside the iron railing that separated them, Iroh loomed like a shadowy figure, his presence both familiar and foreboding. With each tap of his fingers against the metal, it was as though he was punctuating the reality of their situation.

As if sensing her awakening, Iroh addressed her, his voice a low rumble cutting through the silence of the dungeon. "I'm sorry to disturb your rest, Saraphina," he began, his tone laced with concern. "Are you alright?"

Saraphina's response was cold, her voice devoid of its usual warmth. "I've been better," she muttered, her eyes narrowing as she studied Iroh.

Attempting to bridge the gap between them, Iroh explained the dire necessity of their current predicament. "We had to seek refuge here to ensure your safety," he said, his voice tinged with urgency. "It was the only way."

Yet, his words fell upon deaf ears as Saraphina's thoughts stubbornly clung to another name.

With a desperation born of longing, Saraphina whispered the name that echoed in the depths of her soul – Elian. "Where is Elian?" she pleaded, her voice cracking with emotion.

Before the words fully left her lips, Iroh cut her off with a curt retort, his tone as cold and unyielding as the stone that surrounded them. "Elian is not our concern right now," he replied sharply, his eyes hardening.

At that moment, the fragile facade of camaraderie shattered, revealing the stark reality of their fractured alliance. Bound by circumstance yet divided by conflicting loyalties, Saraphina and Iroh stood on opposite sides of an invisible divide.

"And what exactly is our concern, Iroh?" Saraphina challenged, her voice rising with frustration. "Survival? Because last I checked, Elian is integral to that."

In the suffocating confines of the dungeon, the silence that followed spoke volumes. It carried with it the weight of unspoken truths and uncharted paths.

As Iroh's retreating footsteps echoed into the distance, Saraphina found herself alone in the oppressive stillness of the dungeon. Determination set her jaw as she began to survey her surroundings, searching for any possible means of escape. With each passing moment, the walls seemed to close in, the air growing heavier with the weight of confinement.

She tested the bars of her cell, hoping against hope for a weak point, a flaw in the ironwork that she might exploit. But each attempt proved futile, the metal unforgiving beneath her touch. Frustration gnawed at her as she paced the length of her confinement, the dim light casting elongated shadows across the stone floor.

In a desperate bid for freedom, Saraphina attempted to tap into her innate abilities to call upon the power of transformation that had served her well in times of need. But, to her dismay, nothing happened. It was as though her very essence was locked away, inaccessible within the confines of the dungeon.

As she struggled to comprehend the inexplicable blockage, a sudden presence disrupted the solitude of her despair. An unknown figure, cloaked in shadow, materialized before her, his features obscured by darkness.

"You won't find release here, young one," the cloaked stranger spoke, his voice a haunting whisper that sent shivers down Saraphina's spine.

Startled, Saraphina whirled around to face him, her eyes narrowing with suspicion. "Who are you?" she demanded, her voice a mixture of defiance and curiosity.

The stranger offered no immediate answer; instead, he gestured toward the iron bars that imprisoned her. "Your powers are useless within these walls," he explained cryptically. "To transform, to tap into your true potential, you must first leave this place."

Confusion clouded Saraphina's features as she processed his words. "Why?" she pressed, her gaze unwavering.

A knowing smile tugged at the corners of the stranger's lips as he stepped closer, the folds of his cloak swirling around him like a wraith. "This temple is enchanted," he revealed, his voice heavy with ancient secrets. "Every stone, every corridor, resonated with magic older than time itself."

Saraphina's mind raced with newfound understanding, the pieces of the puzzle slotting into place. The realization dawned upon her like the first light of dawn, illuminating the path forward amidst the shadows of uncertainty.

With a newfound resolve, she met the stranger's gaze, her determination burning bright. "Then I'll find a way out," she vowed, her voice echoing with newfound purpose.

As Saraphina stood in the dimly lit dungeon, the cloaked stranger's words pierced through the heavy silence, his voice weighted with the echoes of a forgotten legacy.

"You were the last of the Red Lotus Dragons," he declared, his tone tinged with urgency. "With your power, you could reclaim your birthright as Queen of Draconia, just like your parents before you."

Saraphina's brow furrowed at the mention of her lineage, a mixture of defiance and uncertainty swirling within her. "I don't know," she admitted, her voice tinged with frustration. "And honestly, I don't care about ruling. All I want is to live a happy life."

The stranger's response was sudden and aggressive, his frustration boiling over as he shoved his fists into the iron railing with a force that left a dent in its cold surface.

"You foolish girl!" he growled, his voice laced with anger. "You have a duty, a responsibility to your people. You cannot simply turn your back on your heritage!"

Saraphina recoiled at the sudden outburst, her gaze meeting the stranger's with a mixture of defiance and determination. "My duty is to myself," she retorted, her voice unwavering. "I will not be shackled by the expectations of others."

The tension in the air crackled like lightning, a silent battle of wills unfolding between them. But as the stranger's gaze softened, a flicker of resignation crossing his features, Saraphina knew that she had made her choice.

Saraphina stood in the dimly lit dungeon, her eyes fixed on the cloaked stranger. A shiver ran down her spine as he slowly emerged into the faint light. In the dim glow, she noticed a prominent scar marring his features, slicing across one eye, a jagged reminder of past battles and untold stories.

The sight of the scar triggered a memory buried deep within Saraphina's subconscious, a tale she had stumbled upon in the dusty tomes of ancient lore. In those pages, she had read of a man, a hunter driven by a twisted obsession, his face marked by a similar scar. He was infamous for his merciless pursuit of dragons, driven not by necessity but by sheer pleasure in the hunt.

Fear gripped Saraphina's heart as she realized the gravity of the situation, the implications of the stranger's presence sinking in like an anchor dragging her down. She knew she must tread carefully, for she stood face to face with a predator of legend, a hunter of dragons.

"Why?" she demanded, her voice trembling with a mixture of fear and indignation. "Why did you hunt my kind?"

The stranger met her gaze, his expression unreadable beneath the cloak that shrouded him in darkness. For a moment, the dungeon was filled with silence; only the sounds of their breaths filled the air.

But before he could respond, the stranger retreated into the shadows, leaving Saraphina alone with her unanswered questions. The darkness swallowed him whole, consuming his form until he was nothing more than a fleeting memory, a phantom haunting the depths of her mind.

As Saraphina watched him fade into obscurity, a sense of unease settled over her, a lingering reminder of the danger that lurked in the darkness. For in the stranger's scarred visage, she saw the reflection of a darker truth, a reminder of the shadows that lay beyond the light.

As she stood alone in the dungeon's oppressive silence, she knew that the hunter's legacy lived on, a specter of fear and uncertainty that she could not escape.

***

In the depths of another dungeon, Elian sat alone, the cold stone floor his only companion. His fingers idly traced the contours of a small rock, the monotony of his imprisonment stretching on endlessly.

Suddenly, the heavy silence was shattered by the arrival of Iroh, his presence cutting through the darkness like a beacon of hope. Elian looked up, curiosity flickering in his eyes as he regarded the unexpected visitor.

"Iroh?" he questioned, his voice tinged with surprise.

Iroh wasted no time, his expression grave as he addressed Elian with urgency. "I needed your help," he began, his words carrying a weight of desperation. "I needed you to save her."

Elian's brow furrowed in confusion, his grip tightening on the rock in his hand. "Why would I do that?" he asked, his voice guarded.

A shadow of remorse crossed Iroh's features as he met Elian's gaze, his resolve faltering for a moment. "Because I learned the truth," he confessed, his voice barely above a whisper. "The Council of Dragons, they had other motives. They couldn't allow Dragon Shifters to remain alive, not when their emotions threatened to unleash destruction."

Elian's breath caught in his throat as the gravity of Iroh's words sank in, the realization dawning upon him like a thunderclap. "And you were willing to let me go?" he questioned, disbelief coloring his tone.

Iroh nodded, determination etched into every line of his face. "I will show you a way out," he assured him, his voice tinged with resolve. "There was a back entrance to that dungeon. Lead her out silently and keep her safe."

As Iroh imparted the instructions, Elian's heart pounded with a mixture of apprehension and determination. He knew what had to be done for the sake of Saraphina and all Dragon Shifters like her.

As he prepared to embark on this perilous journey, Elian carried with him the weight of Iroh's revelation, a burden that would shape the course of their destiny. For in the shadows of the dungeon, a new chapter began, fraught with danger and uncertainty, yet illuminated by the flicker of hope.

As Iroh unlocked the heavy gates of Elian's cell, the metallic groan of the hinges echoed through the dimly lit dungeon. Elian's heart raced with a mixture of anticipation and trepidation as he stepped out into the cool, stale air of freedom. Without a word, Iroh gestured for him to go, his eyes reflecting the urgency of their mission.

With a silent nod of gratitude, Elian dashed forward, his footsteps barely making a sound against the cold stone floor. Every movement was calculated, every breath measured as he navigated the labyrinthine corridors of the dungeon.

His senses heightened with adrenaline; Elian remained vigilant, his eyes scanning every shadow for signs of danger. But the silence of the dungeon was deafening, broken only by the faint echo of his own footsteps.

As he neared Saraphina's cell, Elian's heart pounded with a mixture of apprehension and determination. He knew that time was of the essence, that every second wasted brought them closer to danger.

With steady hands, he unlocked the iron bars that imprisoned her, his touch gentle yet urgent. As Saraphina emerged from the darkness, her eyes wide with surprise and relief, Elian offered her a reassuring smile.

In the soft glow of freedom, Saraphina's arms wrapped tightly around Elian, her embrace a testament to the overwhelming relief coursing through her veins. She peppered his face with gentle kisses, each one a silent expression of gratitude and joy.

"Elian," she murmured, her voice trembling with emotion. "I thought I'd never see you again."

Elian returned her embrace with equal fervor, his heart swelling with the warmth of her affection. "Iroh helped me escape," he confessed, his words a whispered revelation against the backdrop of their newfound freedom.

As Saraphina listened, Elian outlined the plan Iroh had shared with him, each detail meticulously planned to ensure their safe passage out of the dungeon and beyond the enchanted walls that had held them captive.

Together, they moved with purpose, their steps synchronized in silent determination. With each passing moment, the weight of their imprisonment faded into memory, replaced by the promise of a future untethered by the chains of the past.

As they emerged into the cool night air, the moonlight bathing them in its silvery glow, Elian and Saraphina shared a silent moment of gratitude.

***

As Elian and Saraphina made their daring escape from the dungeon, their path was suddenly blocked by the unexpected reappearance of the Dragon Hunter. His presence sent a chill down their spines, his menacing silhouette cutting through the darkness like a blade.

"Stop right there," the Hunter commanded, his voice dripping with dangerous authority.

But Saraphina refused to yield, her defiance burning bright in her eyes as she met his gaze head-on. "We're not afraid of you," she retorted, her voice unwavering.

A smirk curled the corners of the Hunter's lips as he regarded them with amusement. "You should be," he warned, his tone laced with a hint of menace.

But Saraphina remained steadfast, her resolve unyielding in the face of his intimidation. "We won't back down," she declared, her voice ringing with defiance.

The Dragon Hunter muttered as he smirked, "Grande Draconia, accorde-moi la sagesse!"

What happened next took them both by surprise. With a muttered incantation, the hunter's form began to shift and warp, his body contorting and elongating until he stood before them in the guise of a magnificent dragon, his scales gleaming a deep, fiery red.

Saraphina's breath caught in her throat as she stared in astonishment at the creature before her, the realization dawning upon her like a thunderclap. "You're... like me," she whispered, her voice filled with wonder and disbelief.

The Dragon Hunter nodded. A smug grin playing across his draconic features. "Indeed," he replied, his voice a low rumble that reverberated through the air. "You are not the only Red Lotus Dragon."

As the truth sank in, Elian and Saraphina exchanged a stunned glance, their minds reeling with the implications of this revelation. For in the depths of the dungeon, amidst the shadows of captivity, they had encountered not only a foe but a kindred spirit bound by the same ancient legacy.

And as they stood face to face with the Dragon Hunter, the air thick with tension and uncertainty, they knew that their journey had only just begun. For beyond the confines of the enchanted walls, a world of mysteries and dangers awaited, where the lines between friend and foe blurred like smoke in the wind.

As the tension between them reached its boiling point, Saraphina's transformation ignited in a blaze of fiery brilliance. Her form shifted and contorted until she stood before them as a magnificent dragon, her scales shimmering with the deep hues of crimson.

With a defiant roar, Saraphina lunged forward, her claws slashing through the air with deadly precision. But the Dragon Hunter was a formidable opponent, his own draconic form a testament to his power and prowess.

Their clash was fierce and relentless, the air crackling with the clash of scales and the roar of flames. But despite Saraphina's courage and determination, she found herself overpowered by the Hunter's relentless assault.

With a heavy thud, Saraphina crashed to the ground, her breath coming in ragged gasps as she struggled to rise. The Dragon Hunter loomed over her, his laughter ringing out like a cruel echo in the night.

Mocking her weakness, the Hunter sneered down at Saraphina, his gaze filled with contempt. But in that moment of vulnerability, Elian rushed to her side, his heart pounding with fear and desperation.

As he embraced Saraphina's wounded form, Elian's hands trembled with the weight of their predicament. The Dragon Hunter watched with a calculating gaze, his smirk twisting into a cruel grin as he savored their despair.

But even in the face of defeat, Elian's love for Saraphina burned bright, a beacon of hope amidst the darkness that threatened to consume them. And as he held her close, he knew that their bond was unbreakable, forged in the crucible of adversity and tested by the fires of battle.

The Dragon Hunter lunged into the scene and grabbed onto Elian as he flew away.

"No! STOP!" Saraphina roared as she slowly got up. She began her flight, trying her best to drag Elian out of it, but the Dragon Hunter hit her several times. He overpowered her and tossed Elian to the ground, but thankfully, Saraphina swung to save him.

"I will take away everything you hold precious," the Hunter roared and smirked.

As she saved him and carried him down slowly, Saraphina's dragon scales began to shimmer and glow with ethereal light, their fiery brilliance intensifying with each passing moment. Her anger got the best of her.

With a fierce roar, Saraphina rose to her feet once more, her form engulfed in a blazing inferno of power and fury. She had transformed into her Mighty Blazing form, a sight to behold as she radiated with the strength of a thousand suns.

With newfound determination, Saraphina launched herself at the Dragon Hunter, her attacks fueled by the flames of vengeance and justice. The air crackled with the intensity of their battle as they clashed with a ferocity that shook the very earth beneath their feet.

Despite the Hunter's formidable strength, Saraphina's Mighty Blazing form proved to be a force to be reckoned with. With each strike, she chipped away at his defenses, her flames searing through his draconic armor with relentless precision.

And then, in a moment of triumph, Saraphina finally overpowered the Dragon Hunter, her flames engulfing him in a blaze of glory. With a triumphant roar, she emerged victorious, her eyes ablaze with the fire of her victory.

With no time to spare, Saraphina swiftly assisted Elian onto her neck, his hands clinging tightly to her scales as they soared into the night sky. Together, they left the chaos of battle behind them, their hearts pounding with the exhilaration of their escape.

As they disappeared into the darkness, leaving the defeated Dragon Hunter far below, Elian and Saraphina knew they had bought themselves precious time. For in the freedom of flight, they found solace and strength, united in their determination to face whatever challenges lay ahead on their journey to redemption.

***

As the flames of battle subsided, the defeated Dragon Hunter underwent a transformation, reverting back to his humanoid form with a mocking laughter that echoed through the night air. His eyes gleamed with a sinister light as he gazed upon Saraphina with a mixture of fascination and malice.

"You were the answer to it all," he declared cryptically, his voice dripping with ominous intent. With a smirk, he rose to his feet, his gaze fixed upon the sky as if plotting his next move.

With a vow that sent a chill down their spines, the Dragon Hunter swore to find Saraphina and end her life, believing her existence to be a threat to the delicate balance of the world. His words hung heavy in the air, a grim reminder of the dangers that lay ahead for Elian and Saraphina.

But their attention was quickly diverted as a group of dragons approached, their expressions grave as they brought Iroh before them. With accusing eyes, they accused him of betrayal, claiming to have found the traitor among them.

Without hesitation, the Dragon Hunter ordered them to throw Iroh back into the dungeon, his voice a cold command that brooked no argument. As the dragons carried out his orders, Iroh's fate hung in the balance, his loyalty called into question amidst the chaos of their world.

And as Elian and Saraphina disappeared into the night sky, their hearts heavy with the weight of uncertainty, they knew that their journey was far from over. In the wake of their escape, a unique story unfolded, fraught with danger and deception, where the line between friend and foe was blurred, and the fate of the world hung in the balance.

Chapter 10: Forever and Always

As Elian and Saraphina soared through the night sky, they could feel the tension slowly dissipating. It was replaced by a sense of relief as they left the chaos of the battle behind them.

"Sara, do you think we'll find safety in that village below?" Elian's voice carried a hopeful tone as he glanced down at the quaint village nestled beneath the trees.

Saraphina nodded, her gaze fixed on the distant lights twinkling through the foliage. "I hope so, Elian. It seems peaceful down there. Perhaps we can find refuge for a while."

With a determined nod, Elian tightened his grip on Saraphina's scales as they descended toward the village, their hearts heavy with the weight of their recent ordeal.

As they reached the outskirts of the village, Elian and Saraphina made their way cautiously through the winding paths, keeping to the shadows as they approached the quaint cottages.

"We must be careful. We can't afford to draw attention to ourselves," Elian whispered, his eyes scanning their surroundings for any signs of danger.

Saraphina nodded in agreement, her senses alert to the slightest sound or movement. "Agreed, Elian. Let's try to blend in as best as we can until we figure out our next move."

With that, they continued, their steps light and cautious as they made their way deeper into the heart of the village.

As they walked through the village square, Saraphina's heart pounded with nervous anticipation. They had barely blended in when a stern voice called out, halting their progress.

"You there, who are you, and what brings you to our village?" The village chief's gaze bore into Saraphina, his expression a mix of suspicion and curiosity.

Saraphina swallowed hard, her mind racing for a suitable explanation. "We're travelers seeking shelter for the night," she replied, her voice steady despite the unease churning in her stomach.

The chief's eyes narrowed as he studied them, his scrutiny unrelenting. "Travelers, you say? And what business do you have in our village?" he pressed in an increasingly demanding tone.

Saraphina exchanged a quick glance with Elian before answering. Her voice was tinged with diplomacy. "We mean no harm, sir. We simply seek respite from our journey and mean to cause no trouble."

The chief's expression softened slightly at her words, but his skepticism remained evident. "Very well, but mark my words, outsiders are not always welcome here. You would do well to remember that."

With a curt nod, Saraphina thanked the chief for his caution. Her mind was already working on their next course of action as they were led to a nearby inn for the night.

As the village chief's gaze lingered on Saraphina's face, a flicker of recognition crossed his features. His eyes widened in astonishment as he studied her closely.

"Saraphina, is it?" The chief's voice was filled with wonder, his tone softening as he addressed her by name. "Forgive my earlier skepticism, but you bear a striking resemblance to someone I once knew."

Saraphina's brow furrowed in confusion, her mind racing to make sense of the chief's words. "I... I don't understand," she stammered, her voice tinged with uncertainty. "I've never been to this village before, and I don't recognize anyone here."

The chief's expression now held an understanding as he placed a comforting hand on Saraphina's shoulder. "No, my dear, I don't expect you to remember. But your resemblance to someone dear to me is uncanny."

With a gentle smile, the chief extended an invitation to Saraphina, his eyes filled with warmth and sincerity. "Please, come with me to my home. There's something I'd like to show you."

Saraphina looked up at him, her confusion giving way to cautious curiosity. "What is it?" she asked, her voice barely above a whisper.

The chief's smile widened as he led Saraphina through the winding streets of the village, his demeanor brimming with excitement. "You'll see," he replied cryptically, his eyes twinkling with anticipation.

As they reached the chief's home, he ushered Saraphina inside, his hands trembling with emotion. With a sense of reverence, he retrieved an old, weathered portrait from a dusty chest; the image faded with time but still holding a profound significance.

Turning to Saraphina, the chief held out the portrait for her to see, his voice trembling with emotion. "This is Delia, my dearest friend," he explained, his eyes shining with unshed tears. "And you... you are the spitting image of her."

Saraphina's heart skipped a beat as she gazed upon the image of her mother, Delia. Tears welled in her eyes as she struggled to comprehend the revelation before her.

"I... I had no idea," Saraphina whispered, her voice choked with emotion. "I never knew my mother, but... but to see her face..."

The chief placed a comforting hand on Saraphina's shoulder, his voice filled with empathy. "You may not have known her, but her spirit lives on in you, Saraphina. You are a part of this village, and we welcome you with open arms."

Saraphina's heart warmed with gratitude as she looked upon the chief with newfound respect. In that moment, she realized that she had found more than just refuge in this village – she had found a connection to her past, a link to the mother she had never known. As she embraced the chief in a heartfelt hug, she knew that she had finally found a place she could call home.

As the night wore on, the village chief gathered the villagers for a solemn ritual, one that had been passed down through generations as a tribute to the Red Lotus Dragons. Saraphina stood at the chief's side, her heart heavy with the weight of the revelations he had shared with her earlier.

"Saraphina," the chief began, his voice carrying across the gathering with quiet reverence. "Tonight, we honor the legacy of your parents, Delia Draconia and Arlong Draconia."

Saraphina's breath caught in her throat as she listened, her mind reeling with the weight of newfound knowledge. She had never known the true extent of her parents' contributions to Draconia nor the profound impact they had left on the village and its people.

"Delia and Arlong were not only beloved leaders of our village, but they were also the embodiment of courage, kindness, and compassion," the chief continued, his words echoing through the stillness of the night. "Their bravery and selflessness were the foundation upon which Draconia was built, and their legacy lives on in each and every one of us."

Tears welled in Saraphina's eyes as she listened to the chief's words, her heart overflowing with pride and gratitude for the parents she had never known. She had always felt a connection to Draconia, but now she understood the true depth of her roots and the profound significance of her heritage.

"As we gather tonight to honor the Red Lotus Dragons, let us also pay tribute to Delia and Arlong, whose sacrifices paved the way for our prosperity and our way of life!" the chief proclaimed, his voice ringing with solemnity. "May their spirits guide us and protect us, now and forevermore."

With that, the villagers bowed their heads in silent reverence, offering their prayers to the heavens above. Saraphina stood among them, her heart brimming with emotion. She felt a sense of belonging that she had never known before. For in the ancient rituals of Draconia, she had found not only a connection to her past but a sense of purpose that would guide her on her journey forward.

As the ritual concluded, the village chief approached Saraphina with a solemn expression, holding out a robe crafted from the fallen scales of the Red Lotus Dragons. "Saraphina, in recognition of your lineage and your presence among us, we offer you this robe," he said with reverence. "May it serve as a symbol of our gratitude for the existence of the Red Lotus Dragons and for your own existence among us."

Saraphina's heart was conflicted with emotions as she accepted the robe, her fingers trembling as she traced the intricate patterns etched into the fabric. She felt overwhelmed by the weight of her heritage, by the sacrifices of her ancestors, and by the expectations placed upon her shoulders.

Unable to bear the weight of it all, Saraphina fled from the village square, tears streaming down her cheeks as she ran. She didn't know where she was going, only that she needed to escape and find solace in the quiet embrace of nature.

Sensing Saraphina's distress, Elian followed after her, his heart heavy with concern. He searched the village frantically, his eyes scanning the surrounding landscape until he spotted her sitting by the edge of a nearby lake, her shoulders shaking with silent sobs.

Approaching her cautiously, Elian knelt beside Saraphina. His presence was a silent comfort in the midst of her turmoil. "Saraphina," he said softly, his voice filled with empathy. "Are you alright?"

Saraphina looked up at him, her eyes red-rimmed and puffy from crying. "Elian," she whispered, her voice choking with emotion. "I don't know if I can do this. The weight of my heritage, of my parents' legacy, it's too much to bear."

Elian placed a gentle hand on her shoulder, his touch warm and reassuring. "You don't have to bear it alone, Saraphina," he said, his voice steady and unwavering. "We're in this together, remember?"

Saraphina nodded, a glimmer of hope flickering in her eyes as she looked at Elian. "Thank you," she said softly in a voice filled with gratitude. "I don't know what I would do without you."

Elian smiled, his heart engulfed with affection for the girl beside him. "You'll never have to find out," he promised, his words a silent vow to always stand by her side, no matter what trials they may face. As they sat together by the edge of the lake, the moonlight casting a soft glow over the water, they found solace in each other's presence. Both of them knew that together, they could weather any storm that came their way.

***

As Elian guided Saraphina back to the village square, the air was heavy with the lingering echoes of the ritual's solemnity. Villagers offered them gentle nods and warm smiles, their peace greetings a silent acknowledgment of the shared bond they now held with Saraphina.

As they entered their appointed room designated by the chief, Saraphina felt a mix of gratitude and trepidation. She knew that she had been welcomed into the village with open arms, yet the weight of her heritage still pressed heavily upon her heart.

Alone in the quiet sanctuary of their room, Saraphina turned to Elian, her eyes reflecting the uncertainty swirling within her. "Elian," she began softly, her voice tinged with vulnerability. "I... I don't know if I can live up to the legacy of my parents, to everything they stood for."

Elian listened intently, his expression one of understanding and empathy. He knew the burden Saraphina carried, the weight of expectations that threatened to overwhelm her. "Saraphina," he said gently, reaching out to take her hand in his. "You don't have to be as strong as your parents. You just have to be yourself."

Saraphina met his gaze, her eyes searching his for reassurance. "But would that be enough? These people expect me to fill in my parents' shoes," she whispered, her voice barely above a breath.

Elian squeezed her hand reassuringly, his touch a silent anchor in the storm of her doubts. "You are more than enough, Saraphina," he said earnestly. "Your parents' legacy lives on in you, but you are your own person, with your own strengths and your own path to forge."

As Saraphina pondered his words, a sense of peace settled over her, the weight of her insecurities gradually lifting from her shoulders. She realized that she didn't have to be a carbon copy of her parents to honor their memory. Her own journey was just beginning, with its own challenges and triumphs waiting to unfold.

With Elian by her side, Saraphina felt a renewed sense of determination, a flicker of hope burning bright within her heart.

As they sat together in the quiet room, their shared bond growing stronger with each passing moment, Saraphina knew that no matter what lay ahead, she would face it with courage and resilience. She felt secure in the knowledge that she was not alone.

Their lips met in a tender kiss, the weight of their shared emotions igniting a passion that had long been dormant. In each other's arms, they found solace and comfort, their bodies entwined in a dance of love and longing.

The night stretched on, filled with whispered words of affection and gentle caresses. It had been too long since they had allowed themselves this intimacy, too long since they had let their love for each other take precedence over the trials and tribulations of their journey.

As Elian broke the kiss with a soft tenderness, he gazed into Saraphina's eyes, his expression filled with adoration and devotion. "I'll love you, forever and always," he murmured, his words a promise that echoed in the depths of her soul.

Saraphina felt her heart swell with overwhelming emotion, tears welling in her eyes as she buried her face in Elian's chest. His declaration of love touched her deeply, reminding her of the unwavering bond they shared, a bond that transcended time and space.

In that moment, surrounded by the warmth of Elian's embrace, Saraphina allowed herself to release the floodgates of her emotions, her sobs mingling with the rhythm of their beating hearts. It was a cathartic release, a testament to the depth of their connection and the strength of their love.

Wrapped in each other's arms, they surrendered to the embrace of the night, finding solace and serenity in the knowledge that no matter what challenges lay ahead, they would face them together, united in a love that was as boundless as the stars above.

As the first light of dawn kissed the horizon, Elian and Saraphina awoke, their fingers intertwined as they basked in the afterglow of their shared intimacy. Saraphina turned to Elian, her eyes searching his with a mixture of uncertainty and longing.

"Elian," she began softly, her voice tinged with vulnerability. "Did you mean what you said last night?"

Elian met her gaze, his expression one of unwavering sincerity. "Of course, Saraphina," he replied earnestly, his voice filled with conviction. "There is no one else in this world who could ever convince me otherwise. You are the love of my life, now and forever."

Saraphina felt emotional, a sense of warmth spreading through her being. In Elian's unwavering devotion, she found reassurance and comfort, knowing that no matter what challenges they may face, they would always have each other.

With a smile, Saraphina shifted closer to Elian, their hands still intertwined as they welcomed the dawn of a new day together. In each other's arms, they found solace and strength, and together, they were ready to face whatever the future held. Elian and Saraphina were united in a love that was as boundless as the sky above.

Chapter 11: The Dragon's Heart

As the weeks turned into months, Elian and Saraphina found themselves deeply rooted in the embrace of the Chief's tribe. The village had become their sanctuary, a haven of peace and tranquility where they could nurture their blossoming love and build a life together.

In the gentle rhythm of village life, Elian and Saraphina's bond grew stronger with each passing day. They shared laughter and tears, dreams, and fears, finding solace and strength in the unwavering support of their newfound family.

Amidst the lush greenery of the village, Elian and Saraphina discovered a sense of belonging they had never known before. They worked side by side with the villagers, tending to the land and embracing the simple joys of communal living.

But amidst the tranquility of their surroundings, a profound realization dawned upon Saraphina. She knew with a certainty that resonated deep within her soul that Elian was the one for her. He was the love she had been searching for all her life.

With her heart overflowing with love and conviction, Saraphina made a decision that would change their lives forever. She approached Elian one evening, under the soft glow of the setting sun, and offered him her hand in marriage.

"Elian," she began, her voice filled with emotion. "I cannot imagine my life without you by my side. Will you marry me?"

Elian's eyes widened in surprise at her heartfelt proposal, but there was no hesitation in his response. With a smile that mirrored the radiance of the sunset, he took Saraphina's hands in his own.

"Yes, Saraphina!" he replied, his voice filled with love and adoration. "I will marry you, for you are my heart, my soul, my everything!"

In that moment, surrounded by the beauty of nature and the warmth of their love, Elian and Saraphina sealed their commitment to each other. It was the start of a journey of love and partnership that would span a lifetime. As they embraced beneath the fading light of the sun, they knew that their love was a bond that could weather any storm. It was a beacon of hope and happiness in a world filled with uncertainty.

On the day of their marriage, the village was alive with excitement and celebration. Elian and Saraphina adorned themselves in traditional tribal attire, their garments vibrant with colors that reflected the richness of their love and the unity of their souls.

As they stood before their loved ones, under the canopy of ancient trees and beneath the endless expanse of the sky, Elian and Saraphina exchanged vows of love and devotion. Their words echoed through the air, a testament to the depth of their commitment and the strength of their bond.

With each promise spoken, their hearts intertwined even further, merging into a single entity bound by the threads of destiny and fate. They pledged to love and cherish each other for all eternity and to support and uplift one another through life's trials and triumphs.

Amidst the cheers and applause of their loved ones, Elian and Saraphina sealed their vows with a kiss, their lips meeting in a tender embrace that spoke volumes of their love and affection. At that moment, they became not just husband and wife, but soulmates united in a love that transcended time and space.

The Chief looked upon them with pride and joy, his heart swelling with happiness at the sight of their union. He approached Saraphina with a warm smile, his eyes sparkling with admiration.

"Saraphina," he said, his voice filled with warmth. "You remind me so much of your mother. She was a woman of strength and grace, just like you."

Saraphina's smile widened at his words, a swell of pride filling her heart. She embraced the Chief in a tight hug, feeling the warmth of his love and acceptance enveloping her like a comforting embrace.

"Thank you, Chief," she replied, her voice tinged with emotion. "Your words mean more to me than you'll ever know."

In that moment, surrounded by the love and support of their village, Elian and Saraphina embarked on a new chapter of their life together. With the blessings of their loved ones and the guidance of their ancestors, they knew that their love would endure, a beacon of hope and happiness in a world filled with uncertainty.

In the soft glow of moonlight filtering through the canopy of trees, Elian and Saraphina surrendered themselves to the depths of their love once more. Their union, already cemented by vows exchanged and hearts intertwined, now took on a new dimension of intimacy and passion.

As they embraced, their bodies pressed together in a symphony of desire and devotion, every touch igniting sparks of passion that danced between them like wildfire. With each movement, they felt the unspoken language of love surging between them, binding them together in a timeless embrace.

Their whispered words of affection echoed through the night, mingling with the gentle rustle of leaves and the symphony of nature's chorus. In the quiet sanctuary of their love, Elian and Saraphina found solace and comfort, their hearts entwined in a dance of ecstasy and euphoria.

As the night wore on, they lost themselves in the rhythm of their love, their bodies moving in perfect harmony as they surrendered to the ecstasy of their union. Time seemed to stand still as they reveled in the beauty of their connection. Their love transcended the boundaries of time and space.

In the quiet moments that followed, as they lay entwined in each other's arms, Elian and Saraphina whispered their love into the stillness of the night. With each tender word spoken, they reaffirmed the depth of their devotion, knowing that their love would endure for all eternity, a beacon of hope and happiness in a world filled with uncertainty.

***

As the morning sun began to cast its gentle rays upon the village, Elian and Saraphina stepped out of their home, greeted by the soothing pattern of raindrops cascading from the heavens.

To their surprise, the Chief was already waiting for them. His wise eyes reflected the wisdom of ages past. He approached them with a warm smile, his presence a reassuring one amidst the tranquil morning.

"Congratulations, my dear friends," he said, his voice filled with genuine warmth and affection. "May your love continue to blossom and flourish like the flowers in spring!"

Elian and Saraphina exchanged grateful smiles, their hearts filled with gratitude for the Chief's kind words. But their reverie was interrupted as the Chief's expression turned serious, his gaze fixed upon Saraphina with unwavering intensity.

"However," he continued, his tone grave yet determined. "I believe it is time for you to undergo training, Saraphina. Not just for yourself, but for the ones you hold dear."

Saraphina's brow furrowed in confusion, her mind racing to grasp the significance of the Chief's words. She knew that training would require dedication and discipline, but she also understood the importance of protecting those she loved with all her heart.

With a solemn nod, she met the Chief's gaze, her determination shining bright in the depths of her eyes. "I understand," she replied, her voice steady and resolute. "I will do whatever it takes to protect my loved ones."

The Chief smiled, a glimmer of pride flickering in his eyes as he witnessed the strength and determination in Saraphina's resolve. "Very well," he said, his voice filled with quiet pride. "Your training begins today, Saraphina, and I will be there every step of the way to guide you."

And so, as the rain continued to fall gently from the sky, Elian and Saraphina took on this new challenge together. With the Chief's guidance and support, they knew that they would face whatever challenges lay ahead with courage and determination, united in their love and their shared commitment to protect the ones they held dear.

As they made their way to the training grounds, Saraphina couldn't help but feel a sense of awe and trepidation as she beheld the Nightshade Reptilian Dragon summoned by the Chief. Its massive form loomed before her, its scales shimmering like polished obsidian in the morning light.

Nemba, as the Chief introduced his dragon, exuded an air of quiet power and majesty. Its eyes, gleaming with intelligence, regarded Saraphina with a sense of curiosity and warmth that belied its fearsome appearance.

Saraphina took a hesitant step forward, her heart pounding with a mixture of excitement and apprehension. The sheer size and strength of Nemba were intimidating, but the Chief's reassuring presence at her side gave her courage.

"It's okay, Saraphina," the Chief said, his voice calm and reassuring. "Nemba is a gentle soul. He's here to help you, to guide you on your journey."

Saraphina nodded, her gaze still fixed on the magnificent creature before her. With the Chief's words echoing in her mind, she took a tentative step closer to Nemba, extending a trembling hand toward his massive form.

To her surprise, Nemba responded with a gentle nuzzle, his warm breath washing over her like a comforting embrace.

Saraphina instantly felt a sense of connection with the dragon, one she couldn't put into words.

With the Chief's guidance, Saraphina began her training alongside Nemba, learning the ways of combat and strategy under the watchful eye of her newfound mentor. As she forged a deeper bond with the dragon by her side, she realized that with courage and determination, she could overcome any obstacle that stood in her path.

Under Nemba's patient guidance, Saraphina embraced her transformation with newfound confidence. With each training session, she honed her fighting skills, soaring to dizzying heights under the watchful eye of her mentor. She felt the rush of wind against her scales, the freedom of the open skies empowering her with a sense of exhilaration she had never known before.

Controlling her fire breath proved to be a more daunting challenge, but with Nemba's encouragement and expertise, Saraphina gradually gained mastery over this elemental power. She learned to channel the flames with precision and control, unleashing bursts of fire with a focused determination that left even Nemba impressed.

Yet, it was Nemba's insistence on unlocking her true potential that truly pushed Saraphina to her limits. With each passing day, he urged her to delve deeper into herself, to tap into the power that lay dormant within her.

As she trained under Nemba's guidance, Saraphina's Mighty Blazing Form emerged not as a last resort but as a beacon of power and resilience. With each transformation, she felt the surge of raw energy coursing through her veins, her flames burning brighter and hotter than ever before.

With Nemba's unwavering support, Saraphina embraced her true potential, embracing her role as protector of the tribe and guardian of Draconia's legacy. As she soared through the skies with Nemba by her side, she knew that together, they would face whatever challenges lay ahead with courage and determination, united in their quest for greatness.

As Elian watched Saraphina and Nemba engage in their training, a smile spread across his face, filled with pride and admiration. Seeing his wife harnessing her newfound powers with such grace and determination filled him with awe and wonder.

The sight of Saraphina, her form ablaze with the fierce flames of her Mighty Blazing Form, was a testament to her strength and resilience. Her transformation was more than just a display of power; it was a symbol of her unwavering commitment to protect those she loved.

As Saraphina and Nemba clashed in the air, their movements fluid and precise, Elian couldn't help but marvel at their beauty. It was a sight to behold, a testament to the deep bond shared between dragon and rider.

With each passing moment, Elian's love for Saraphina grew stronger, and his heart filled with pride at the incredible woman she had become. He knew that with her by his side, they could face any challenge that lay ahead, their bond unbreakable and their love enduring.

As the training session came to an end, Elian approached Saraphina with a smile, his eyes shining with admiration. "You were amazing," he said, his voice filled with warmth and affection. "I'm so proud of you, my love."

Chapter 12: Into the Fire

With each passing day, Saraphina immersed herself deeper into her training, embracing the relentless pursuit of mastery over her powers. Under the watchful guidance of Nemba and the Chief, she learned the importance of discipline and control, honing her skills with unwavering determination.

The training sessions became more intense as Saraphina pushed herself to new limits, testing the boundaries of her strength and endurance. She practiced tirelessly, refining her techniques and perfecting her control over her elemental abilities.

At first, there were moments of frustration and doubt as Saraphina grappled with the immense power that coursed through her veins. But with each setback, she persevered and channeled her determination as fuel for her growth.

Nemba was a constant source of encouragement and guidance; his wisdom and experience guided Saraphina through the challenges she faced. He taught her to harness the raw energy within her, to temper it with focus and precision.

As Saraphina delved deeper into her training, she began to understand the true importance of control. She learned to channel her fiery temperament with patience and restraint, mastering the art of keeping her powers in check even in the heat of the battle.

With each passing day, Saraphina's confidence grew, her movements becoming more fluid and precise. She learned to trust in her instincts and rely on her training, knowing that with discipline and control, she could overcome any obstacle that came her way.

As she continued to train relentlessly, Saraphina knew that she was on the path to greatness. Her determination remained unwavering as she embraced her destiny as protector of the tribe and guardian of Draconia's legacy.

With time, as Saraphina's training progressed, she began to notice subtle changes within herself. Her powers seemed to be growing exponentially, expanding beyond her control. She felt the raw energy within her surging to new heights, becoming a potent force waiting to be unleashed.

One night, as she and Elian shared a moment of intimacy, Saraphina felt her emotions swell within her, overflowing like a torrential wave. In the heat of the moment, her powers surged uncontrollably, overwhelming her senses and consuming her in a blaze of fiery energy.

In an instant, Saraphina transformed, her body engulfed in the radiant glow of her Mighty Blazing Form. Flames danced around her, illuminating the darkness with their brilliant light as she struggled to regain control.

Elian watched in awe as his wife underwent this unexpected transformation, his heart pounding with a mixture of fear and fascination. He reached out to her, his touch a comforting anchor amidst the chaos of her power.

With each passing moment, Saraphina fought to reign in her unruly abilities and to quell the raging inferno that threatened to consume her. It was only through sheer force of will that she gradually regained control, her flames subsiding as she returned to her human form.

Exhausted but exhilarated, Saraphina collapsed into Elian's arms, her chest heaving with exertion as she caught her breath. She looked up at him, her eyes filled with a mixture of awe and uncertainty.

"I... I didn't mean for that to happen," she whispered, her voice trembling with emotion. "I lost control."

Elian held her close, his arms a comforting embrace as he reassured her. "It's okay," he murmured, his voice gentle and soothing. "We'll figure it out together."

As they held each other beneath the starlit sky, Elian and Saraphina knew that they would face whatever challenges lay ahead as one, their love and devotion guiding them through the trials that awaited.

***

The next morning, Saraphina sought out the Chief, her mind still reeling from the events of the previous night. She found him standing at the edge of the training grounds, his gaze fixed on the horizon as he contemplated the new challenges they faced.

Approaching him with a sense of trepidation, Saraphina greeted the Chief with a respectful nod. "Chief," she began, her voice tinged with uncertainty. "About last night..."

The Chief turned to face her, his expression grave yet understanding. "I saw what happened," he said, his tone solemn. "Your powers are growing stronger, but they are also becoming more unpredictable."

Saraphina's heart sank at his words, the weight of their implications settling heavily upon her shoulders. She knew that her newfound abilities could pose a danger not only to herself but to those she cared about.

"I don't want to hurt anyone," she confessed, her voice barely above a whisper. "But I don't know how to control it."

The Chief placed a reassuring hand on her shoulder, his touch a comforting presence amidst her turmoil. "It won't be easy," he admitted. "But we will help you. Together, we will find a way to harness your power and keep those around you safe."

Saraphina nodded, a sense of determination igniting within her. She knew that mastering her abilities would be a daunting task, but she was willing to do whatever it took to protect those she loved.

As she and the Chief discussed plans for her training, Saraphina felt a glimmer of hope amidst the uncertainty. With the Chief's guidance and support, she knew that she could face the challenges ahead with courage and resilience. With Elian by her side, she felt confident that together, they could overcome any obstacle that stood in their way.

Saraphina looked up at the Chief, her eyes reflecting a mix of determination and gratitude. "Thank you, Chief," she said sincerely. "I won't let you down. I'll do whatever it takes to learn control."

The Chief offered her a reassuring smile. "I have faith in you, Saraphina," he replied. "But remember, it's not just about controlling your powers. It's also about understanding them, embracing them as a part of who you are."

His words resonated with Saraphina, reminding her that her abilities were not something to be feared but rather a gift to be cherished and honed. "I understand," she affirmed, her voice steady. "I'll approach this with an open mind and a willing heart."

With a nod of approval, the Chief gestured toward the training grounds. "Let's begin," he said, his tone resolute. "We'll start by focusing on meditation and breath control. It's the foundation of mastering your powers."

As they walked toward the training area, Saraphina felt a sense of anticipation building within her. She knew that the road ahead would be challenging, but she also knew that with the Chief's guidance and support, she had the strength to face whatever lay ahead.

***

In the depths of an abandoned cave, a silhouette sat hunched over, his form obscured by the shadows that danced across the walls. With each bite of his meal, he muttered incantations under his breath, his voice a low murmur that reverberated through the cavern.

As he finished his meal, the figure's attention shifted to the task at hand. With a flick of his wrist, he produced a tattered scroll from within the folds of his cloak, its surface adorned with arcane symbols and markings.

Unfurling the scroll, he traced his finger along the ancient script, his eyes narrowing with focus as he marked his next target. It was the Dragon Hunter, a notorious figure known for his relentless pursuit of dragons and those with draconian blood.

With a grim determination, the figure muttered a final incantation, sealing the fate of his next quarry. The scroll ignited in a flash of ethereal light before disintegrating into ash, leaving behind only the lingering echo of his dark intentions.

As he rose from his seat, the figure donned his cloak once more, the fabric billowing around him like a shroud of darkness. With purposeful strides, he vanished into the depths of the cave, his steps guided by the promise of bounty and the thrill of the hunt.

***

During one of Saraphina's rigorous training sessions, as she soared through the sky under Nemba's watchful eye, the Chief's urgent call echoed through the air, breaking the rhythm of her flight. Startled, she descended to the ground, her heart pounding with anticipation and a hint of apprehension.

With a quick exchange of glances with Elian, who stood nearby, Saraphina approached the Chief; her brow furrowed with concern. "Is everything alright?" she inquired, her voice laced with urgency.

The Chief's expression was grave as he met her gaze. "There's something you need to know," he began, his voice commanding attention. "The Dragon Hunter's presence has been detected near the outskirts of our territory."

As the Chief spoke of the thief who stole the powers of the Red Lotus Dragon, Saraphina's heart sank with dread. The thought of someone wielding such immense power for their own selfish desires sent shivers down her spine.

Beside her, Elian sensed her unease and placed a comforting hand on her shoulder. "We'll face this threat together," he whispered, his voice a soothing balm to her frayed nerves.

With Elian's support, Saraphina found the courage to voice her concerns to the Chief. "Who is this Dragon Hunter?" she asked, her voice trembling slightly with a mixture of fear and determination.

The Chief's expression darkened as he spoke of the infamous figure. "The Dragon Hunter is a cunning and ruthless adversary," he explained. "He seeks to harness the powers of dragons for his own gain, regardless of the consequences."

Elian's jaw tightened with resolve as he listened to the Chief's words. "We cannot allow him to succeed," he declared, his tone firm and unwavering.

The Chief nodded in agreement. "Indeed," he replied. "We must remain vigilant and prepared to defend ourselves against any threat that may arise."

With a shared understanding of the danger they faced, Saraphina and Elian redoubled their efforts in their training. Each day, they pushed themselves to new heights, honing their skills and preparing for the inevitable confrontation with the Dragon Hunter.

As they continued to train, a sense of determination burned within them, driving them forward in their quest to protect their loved ones and safeguard the legacy of the Red Lotus Dragon. With the Chief's guidance and Elian's unwavering support, Saraphina knew that together, they would stand strong against the darkness that threatened to engulf them.

Saraphina's focus was unwavering, her determination driving her to push her limits further each day. She and Nemba, the Chief's Nightshade Reptilian Dragon, had forged a strong bond during their training, and under Nemba's guidance, Saraphina's skills had grown exponentially.

As they practiced controlling her fire breath and mastering aerial maneuvers, Saraphina's senses remained sharp, attuned to every movement and sound in the surrounding forest. It was during one such training session that she noticed a disturbance in the sky above.

Pausing mid-flight, Saraphina's gaze was drawn to a distant flock of dragons soaring gracefully through the clouds. Their majestic forms painted a striking silhouette against the azure canvas of the sky; their wings outstretched as they glided effortlessly through the air.

The sight of the approaching dragon flock sent a shiver down Saraphina's spine, her heart racing with a mixture of fear and uncertainty. Beside her, Elian tensed, his eyes narrowing as he assessed the situation.

With a sense of urgency, the Chief urged them to take cover, his voice a commanding presence amidst the chaos that threatened to engulf their tribe. "Quickly, find shelter," he instructed, his tone edged with urgency.

Saraphina's mind raced as she scanned their surroundings, searching for a safe haven amidst the looming threat. With a swift nod to Elian, they darted toward the nearest cluster of trees, their footsteps echoing in the air as they sought refuge from the impending danger.

As they crouched behind the dense foliage, their breaths came in ragged gasps, adrenaline coursing through their veins while they awaited the arrival of the dragons. Saraphina's fingers trembled with nervous energy, her senses heightened to the slightest sound or movement.

Above them, the air thrummed with the beating of wings as the dragon flock descended upon the tribe, their majestic forms casting ominous shadows against the sky. Saraphina held her breath, her heart pounding in her chest as she prayed for their safety amidst the chaos.

Through the branches, they watched in tense silence as the dragons circled above, their keen eyes scanning the area with a sense of purpose. The Chief's tribe remained hidden, their presence concealed from the watchful gaze of the dragons as they waited for the threat to pass.

Minutes stretched into eternity as Saraphina and Elian huddled together, their hearts pounding in unison with the rhythm of the forest. With each passing moment, the tension in the air grew thicker, suffocating them with the weight of uncertainty.

But just as suddenly as they had appeared, the dragons soared away into the distance, their departure leaving a sense of relief in their wake. Saraphina exhaled a shaky breath, her shoulders sagging with the release of tension as she realized they had narrowly escaped disaster once more.

Chapter 13: A Battle of Wills

As the weeks passed, Saraphina's training intensified, each day bringing new challenges and triumphs. Under the watchful guidance of the Chief and Nemba, she honed her skills and mastered her powers with unwavering dedication.

One morning, as Saraphina and Elian enjoyed a quiet moment together, the Chief approached them with a solemn expression on his face. His eyes held a mixture of pride and determination as he spoke to Saraphina.

"Saraphina, the time has come," he announced, his voice carrying the weight of their shared journey. "You are now ready."

Saraphina's heart swelled with a mixture of excitement and apprehension at the Chief's words.

Turning to Elian, she met his gaze with determination. "We need to head to Mount Bliss," she told him, her voice filled with conviction. "It's where all the Red Lotus Dragons join together for their meetings. If there's any chance of uncovering the truth about the Dragon Hunter and his motives, that's where we'll find it."

Elian nodded in agreement, his eyes reflecting the same determination as Saraphina's. Together, they prepared for the journey ahead, their hearts set on uncovering the secrets that lay hidden in the heart of the mountains.

With heartfelt gratitude, Saraphina and Elian bid farewell to the Chief and the tribe, their spirits buoyed by the Chief's wisdom and support. As they embarked on the path toward Mount Bliss, a sense of anticipation mingled with the natural beauty of their surroundings.

The forest came alive with the sights and sounds of mystical creatures, their presence a testament to the ancient magic that permeated the land. Vibrant flora adorned the forest floor while ethereal creatures flitted through the canopy above, their iridescent wings casting shimmering patterns of light.

Saraphina and Elian marveled at the wonders around them, each encounter with a mystical creature filling them with awe and wonder. They encountered playful sprites dancing among the trees, wise old ents guarding ancient groves, and majestic unicorns grazing in sunlit clearings.

With each step, Saraphina and Elian felt a deep connection to the natural world, serving as a reminder of the importance of preserving the delicate balance of life. Amidst the beauty and serenity of the forest, they found solace and strength, their bond growing stronger with each shared moment.

As they journeyed onward, the path ahead seemed to shimmer with the promise of adventure and discovery. With determination in their hearts and the guidance of the Chief's teachings, Saraphina and Elian pressed forward, ready to face whatever challenges lay ahead in their quest for truth and justice.

***

As Saraphina and Elian continued their journey toward Mount Bliss, they stumbled upon a clearing bathed in golden sunlight. There, before them, a flock of majestic phoenixes took flight, their fiery plumage trailing behind them like a cascade of flames.

Saraphina's eyes widened in awe at the sight, her heart swelling with admiration for the magnificent creatures before her. She turned to Elian, her excitement palpable as she gestured toward the soaring phoenixes.

"Did you see that, Elian?!" she exclaimed, her voice tinged with wonder. "Their tails, they're like... like blazing infernos! Can you imagine being able to do that?"

Elian smiled warmly at Saraphina's enthusiasm, his eyes reflecting her sense of awe. "It's incredible, isn't it?" he voiced his admiration. "While I can't quite match the majesty of a phoenix, I have my own ways of harnessing the power of fire."

"And how might that be?" Saraphina smiled in amazement as she stood next to him and folded her arms.

"Uh... Well," Elian scoffed and scratched his head. But Saraphina kissed his cheek and took him back toward their trail. As they watched the phoenixes disappear into the horizon, Saraphina couldn't shake the feeling of inspiration that welled up within her. With each beat of their fiery wings, she felt a renewed determination to unlock the full extent of her own abilities, soar to new heights, and embrace her destiny as a Red Lotus Dragon.

As Saraphina and Elian ventured deeper into the wilderness, the air seemed to hum with the presence of magic, and each step brought them closer to the heart of the mystical realm.

Together, they made their way through the enchanting landscape. Amidst the wonders of the wilderness, they found solace and comfort in each other's presence, their love a beacon of light in the darkness.

As they journeyed onward, their hearts filled with a sense of adventure and anticipation, knowing that each encounter brought them closer to their destination. With every passing moment, they felt more connected to the magic that surrounded them and to each other.

***

As Saraphina and Elian drew closer to the imposing peak of Mount Bliss, a cold dread seeped into their hearts. Atop a large rock at the mountain's base, they spotted The Dragon Hunter, his imposing figure silhouetted against the clear sky. He sat in deep meditation, an air of menace radiating from him that spread like a dark fog, shrouding their path in uncertainty.

Suddenly, The Dragon Hunter's eyes snapped open, gleaming with a malevolent fire. With a menacing jerk, he rose to his full height, his gaze fixed upon Saraphina. His voice, laced with cruel amusement, boomed across the valley, "This day marks the end of your tyranny, Red Lotus Dragon! Your fiery breath will soon fuel my own power, making me the mightiest dragon to ever grace the skies!"

Saraphina, however, remained undeterred. Her eyes, usually warm and inviting, now blazed with defiance as she met his hateful stare. A steely resolve settled in her voice as she countered, "Your threats are hollow, Dragon Hunter! If you seek a battle, then so be it. I am ready to face you."

Elian's brow furrowed with worry. Reaching out, he placed a comforting hand on her shoulder. "Saraphina," he cautioned, his voice tight with concern, "underestimate him at your peril. He is far more dangerous than he seems."

Saraphina offered him a reassuring nod. She straightened her posture, steeling herself for the inevitable confrontation. The coming battle promised to be brutal, but she wouldn't falter. For the sake of her loved ones and for the future of Draconia, she would emerge victorious.

As Saraphina's defiant words hung heavy in the air, a surge of energy crackled around her. Her body shimmered and contorted, scales erupting from her skin and her limbs elongating. With a mighty roar that echoed through the valley, Saraphina transformed into her magnificent Red Lotus Dragon form. Crimson scales, the color of a burning sunset, shimmered in the sunlight, and enormous wings, like tattered sails of fire, unfurled behind her.

The Dragon Hunter, mirroring her transformation, let out a guttural roar that shook the very mountain. His form twisted and warped, dark scales replacing leathery armor, and powerful wings, like obsidian blades, erupted from his back. He towered over Saraphina, a monstrous obsidian dragon with eyes that burned like embers.

The fight erupted in a whirlwind of claws, fangs, and fire. Saraphina, lighter and faster on her wings, danced around the lumbering Dragon Hunter. Their clash was a spectacle of raw power. With each swipe of her claws, she tore furrows into the mountainside, sending cascades of rock tumbling down. The Dragon Hunter countered with brute force, his massive tail slamming into the mountain with earth-shattering force, creating tremors that forced Elian to scramble for safety.

The Dragon Hunter unleashed a torrent of white-hot flames in a wave of searing heat that engulfed the mountain peak. But Saraphina, with a powerful beat of her wings, launched herself into the air, narrowly avoiding the inferno. From above, she swooped down, her claws a blur of red as she raked them across the Dragon Hunter's arm, drawing a spray of molten black ichor.

The Dragon Hunter roared in pain and fury, the sound echoing through the valley like thunder. He whipped his head around, snapping his jaws at the airborne Saraphina, but she was already a blur of crimson. The fight was far from over.

Saraphina's crimson form danced a deadly ballet as she evaded the Dragon Hunter's counterattack. The swipe of his massive tail missed her by inches, but the shockwave from the attack sent a tremor through the mountain, ripping loose a huge chunk of rock that slammed into her side. With a pained shriek, Saraphina lost altitude and careened into the mountainside, scales scraping raw against the rough stone.

Elian, rooted to the spot just a moment before, surged forward with a roar of frustration. He couldn't stand by and watch the woman he loved be brutalized. Spotting his bow and arrows propped against a nearby rock, he lunged for them with a desperation that fueled his movements. As Saraphina crashed, momentarily stunned, Elian drew his bow back, nocking an arrow imbued with ancient enchantments. The air crackled with magic as he aimed. The arrow, tipped with a shimmering stone that pulsed with blue energy, left the bow in a blur.

The Dragon Hunter, momentarily distracted by Saraphina's fall, turned his massive head just in time to see the enchanted arrow streak toward him. It struck true, piercing his obsidian-like scales with a sickening thud. A jolt of blue energy erupted from the point of impact, coursing through the Dragon Hunter's body. He roared in fury and pain, thrashing his head, the force of his struggles temporarily dislodging the arrow.

This diversion gave Saraphina a precious moment to recover. A surge of adrenaline masked the throbbing pain in her side as she pushed herself off the mountainside with renewed vigor. The sight of Elian's bravery, his willingness to face a creature far beyond his capabilities, filled her with fierce determination. She wouldn't let his sacrifice be in vain.

With a powerful beat of her wings, she launched herself back into the fray. The Dragon Hunter, still reeling from the enchanted arrow, was caught off guard by her sudden attack. She dove toward him, her claws extended, aiming for his exposed underbelly, the one chink in his seemingly impenetrable armor. This was her chance, a gamble she had to take.

The wind roared in Saraphina's ears as she plummeted toward the Dragon Hunter.

With a burst of speed, Saraphina angled herself perfectly, aiming for the soft underbelly exposed by the Dragon Hunter's contortions. Her fiery claws, honed to a razor's edge, glinted in the sunlight as they tore through the leathery hide in a spray of sparks and black ichor. A monstrous screech split the air as the Dragon Hunter lurched backward, the impact of Saraphina's attack sending him crashing into the mountainside.

A plume of dust and debris erupted, momentarily obscuring the scene. Saraphina circled cautiously, her breaths ragged, the pain in her side a dull throb now. The dust settled, revealing the Dragon Hunter, a monstrous figure half-buried in the rocks. His scales were marred by a deep gash, and the enchanted arrow still protruded from his side, pulsing faintly with blue energy.

He let out a low growl, a sound that vibrated through the earth, filled with a primal fury and a hint of something else – fear. It was a sound Saraphina had never heard from a dragon before. It ignited a spark of hope within her.

"Yield, Dragon Hunter!" she boomed, her voice echoing across the valley. "Your reign of terror ends here."

The Dragon Hunter struggled to his feet, a monstrous silhouette against the clear sky. His eyes, once burning embers, now flickered with desperation. He opened his maw, ready to unleash another torrent of flames, but hesitated. The weakness from the enchanted arrow coursed through his veins, sapping his strength.

"You cannot defeat me, Red Lotus!" he roared, his voice strained. "I am destined to become the ultimate dragon!"

Saraphina narrowed her eyes. His words hinted at a deeper purpose, a reason for his relentless pursuit of power. Could there be more to him than just a mindless tyrant? Perhaps a twisted sense of duty fueled by a dark prophecy or a broken oath. But regardless of his motivations, she wouldn't let him jeopardize the peace of Draconia.

"Then your destiny ends now!" she declared, readying herself for another attack. But before she could launch herself into the fray, a loud crack echoed from above. She looked up to see a massive piece of mountainside, dislodged by the earlier battle, teetering precariously.

In a split second, realization dawned on her. The Dragon Hunter, weakened and cornered, was a threat, but the real danger now stemmed from the falling rock. It wouldn't just crush the Dragon Hunter; it could bury Elian, who was still huddled at the foot of the mountain.

A surge of protectiveness overwhelmed Saraphina. Without hesitation, she dived downwards, pushing past the searing pain in her side. She had to reach Elian to get him out of harm's way, even if it meant leaving the Dragon Hunter to his fate.

Chapter 14: The Final Showdown

Saraphina skidded to a halt beside Elian, the thunderous crash of the rocks nearly drowning out the pounding in her ears. Dust choked the air, momentarily obscuring their vision. Elian clung to her arm and began to cough. As the dust cleared, they both looked toward the spot where the Dragon Hunter had stood.

A mangled mess of stone and wood pinned him down. The emerald gleam of scales was gone, replaced by ripped hunter's leathers and a glimpse of pale skin. The Dragon Hunter had shifted back into his human form.

Relief washed over Saraphina, quickly followed by a pang of something unexpected. He was injured, maybe even unconscious. A primal urge to help stirred within her.

"Stay here," she instructed Elian, her voice hoarse. Despite the throbbing pain in her side, she lumbered toward the fallen rock face. The air hung heavy with the metallic tang of blood.

"Don't touch me, you beast!" A strained voice ripped through the suffocating silence. The Dragon Hunter lay beneath a heavy beam, his face contorted in pain. Fear flickered in his eyes, but it was quickly replaced by a fierce defiance when he saw Saraphina approaching.

She stopped, torn between her instincts and the venom in his voice. "You're hurt. Let me help you."

"I'd rather rot here than owe my life to your kind!" he spat, his voice laced with both pain and disgust.

Saraphina clenched her jaw. The irony wasn't lost on her. He was the hunter, yet here he was the prey. Yet, she couldn't leave him to die.

"Fine," she said, her voice clipped. "But don't expect gratitude."

Heaving with effort, she wedged her powerful claws beneath the fallen beam, pushing upwards with a surge of dragon strength. The groan of wood protested, slowly giving way. Relief flickered across the Hunter's face, momentarily replacing the animosity.

With a final heave, she managed to free him. He collapsed onto the dirt, gasping for breath. Saraphina watched him warily, her own injuries screaming at her. There was a tense silence between them – a predator sizing up its wounded prey.

The Dragon Hunter finally spoke, his voice raspy. "Thanks," he muttered, the word grudgingly escaping his lips.

Saraphina snorted. "Consider it a debt repaid. Your trap nearly got Elian killed."

He flinched at the mention of the boy. "What did you..."

"Enough talk," she interrupted, her voice weary. "We need to get out of here before more falls."

She glanced at Elian, who was watching them with wide, worried eyes. Saraphina knew they wouldn't get far with the Hunter injured. An idea sparked within her, fueled by desperation and a strange sense of obligation.

"Hold on," she said, turning to the Hunter. "You can barely stand. I can…" She hesitated, loathing the suggestion. "I can carry you, but it has to be on my terms."

The Dragon Hunter's eyes narrowed. This was a precarious truce, and neither of them knew if it would hold.

The air crackled with tension as Saraphina awaited the Hunter's response. Their uneasy alliance hung in the balance, the weight of their mutual distrust a heavy burden. Suddenly, a ragged figure emerged from the cloud of dust billowing from the fallen rocks.

The newcomer was cloaked from head to toe, his form obscured by the tattered fabric. He moved with a slow, deliberate gait, his presence sending a shiver down Saraphina's spine. As he drew closer, a glint of golden light pierced through a slit in the cloak, revealing a single, watchful eye.

"Saraphina," the figure rasped, his voice a gravelly whisper. Recognition dawned on her in a flash. It was Veridan, a high-ranking member of the Dragon Council, the very organization that had branded her a fugitive.

His arrival shattered the fragile truce between her and the Hunter. Veridan gestured toward the dust-filled horizon. A low rumble echoed from afar, growing steadily louder. Saraphina squinted through the haze and gasped. A squadron of dragons, their scales glinting in the afternoon sun, soared toward them in a coordinated formation.

"Your reign of terror ends here, Dragon Shifter," Veridan declared, his voice laced with a chilling authority. "The Council has deemed you a danger to the realm. Stand down and surrender peacefully."

Panic clawed at Saraphina's throat. The Council had mobilized with terrifying speed. She glanced at the Hunter, who watched the approaching dragons with a mixture of apprehension and what might have been grudging respect.

"This is insane," she growled at Veridan. "I haven't done anything wrong!"

"Your defiance is proof enough," he countered. "You have defied the Council's authority and unleashed chaos upon the land. Now face the consequences."

Saraphina's gaze darted between the approaching dragons and the injured Hunter. Trapped between two formidable forces, fury coursed through Saraphina, incinerating the remnants of her strained alliance with the Hunter.

"Chaos?" she roared, her voice echoing through the canyon. "It was your doing! You, the Council, who sowed the seeds of this discord with your fear and persecution! I, a lone shifter, am labeled a threat for defending myself?"

The approaching dragons formed a tight circle overhead, casting their elongated shadows upon the ground. Veridan remained impassive, his single visible eye glinting with cold authority.

With a sickening thud, two figures were unceremoniously dumped at Saraphina's feet. Elian, his face pale and streaked with tears, looked up at her with a mixture of fear and defiance. But it was the other figure that truly stole her breath. Iroh, her old friend and fierce protector, lay crumpled beside him, blood staining his once-gleaming armor.

A primal scream ripped from Saraphina's throat, a sound that shook the very stones of the canyon. Grief and rage warred within her, threatening to consume her. Veridan's words seemed to echo in the deafening silence that followed.

"Give it up, Saraphina," he said, his voice dripping with a false sense of sympathy. "Fighting is futile. You are a danger to yourself and everyone around you. Accept your fate."

But acceptance was the furthest thing from Saraphina's mind. Instead, a surge of power unlike anything she'd ever experienced coursed through her veins. Veridan's words were a twisted mockery, a justification for their tyranny. She wouldn't be a pawn in their game any longer.

With a guttural roar that sent tremors through the earth, the ground beneath Saraphina cracked and shifted. A blinding flash of light erupted, engulfing her in a swirling vortex of fire and energy. The onlookers shielded their eyes as Saraphina's form contorted and reshaped. When the light finally subsided, a magnificent dragon stood before them.

Scales the color of molten gold shimmered in the afternoon sun, each flake glowing with an intensity that outshone even the dragons of the Council. The air crackled with raw power, revealing the depth of Saraphina's fury. The Dragon Hunter watched in stunned silence, never before witnessing flames so vibrant and potent.

This wasn't just a transformation – it was a declaration of war.

Saraphina's roar tore through the canyon, a primal challenge that echoed off the mountains. Her wings, vast and powerful, beat against the air, creating a gale that whipped sand and debris into a frenzy. The Council Dragons, for all their training and discipline, faltered in the face of her incandescent rage.

Their fire seemed dull in comparison to hers. She was a storm unleashed, weaving through their ranks with a terrifying grace. With a snap of her jaws, she disarmed one dragon, sending him tumbling from the sky. Another charged, claws bared, only to be met with a searing blast of fire that singed his wings and sent him crashing into a nearby rock face.

Meanwhile, the Dragon Hunter, giving way to action, saw his opportunity. He sprinted toward Elian and Iroh, dodging falling debris from the fray above him. Using his remaining strength, he hoisted the unconscious Iroh onto his back and scooped Elian into his arms.

"This way!" he yelled, leading Elian toward some hidden crevices in the rocks. The boy stumbled along, fear etched on his face, but he didn't hesitate to follow.

From above, Saraphina saw the Hunter's actions. A flicker of surprise momentarily cooled her rage. Was he repaying his debt, defying the Council alongside her? It didn't matter. Right now, their goal was the same — to protect the innocent.

With renewed ferocity, she tore through the remaining Council Dragons. Their coordinated attack had become a desperate scramble for survival. One by one, they fell, either scorched by her fire or forced to retreat. The air grew heavy with the metallic scent of blood and burning scales.

Finally, only Veridan remained. He hovered above the carnage, and his single eye narrowed in what could have been fear or respect. Saraphina landed with a thunderous crash, the earth trembling under her weight.

She roared a challenge, a promise. This wasn't over. The Council's reign of terror would end, replaced by a future where Dragon Shifters could exist in peace. Veridan remained silent, his motives shrouded in that watchful eye.

The echo of her roar faded, replaced by an unsettling silence. Saraphina willed herself back into her human form, her rage simmering beneath the surface. The transformation was agonizing and left her drained and shaky, but the vulnerability felt empowering. She snatched a discarded cloak from a fallen Council member, draping it around her naked body.

Veridan remained suspended in the air, his singular eye a beacon of unsettling intensity. Her voice, though raspy, held the weight of her newfound power.

"You've lost, Veridan!" she declared, each word a hammer blow. "Leave this place. Leave my family and me alone." She knelt beside Iroh, checking for a pulse. Relief flooded her when she found it, weak but steady.

"Consider this a warning," she continued, her gaze unwavering as it met Veridan's. "If a single hair on their heads is harmed, the Council you hold so dear will crumble under the flames of my fury. You've seen what I'm capable of. Don't tempt fate again."

Veridan studied her for a long, tense moment. Perhaps he saw the raw power that still crackled around her. It was a constant reminder of her devastating transformation. Or perhaps he saw the fierce protectiveness that burned brighter than any fire.

Whatever his reason, Veridan bowed his head in a gesture that could be interpreted as either submission or calculation. With a powerful beat of his wings, he turned and disappeared into the distance, his entourage of fallen dragons a grim testament to Saraphina's victory.

Exhaustion crashed over her, pulling at her weakened form. But as she secured Iroh more comfortably and looked at Elian's tear-streaked face, a surge of determination coursed through her.

This wasn't just a victory; it was a turning point. The fight for a future where Dragon Shifters could live freely had just begun. Saraphina, forever changed by fire and fury, was ready to lead the charge. The path ahead wouldn't be easy, but with Elian safe and Iroh by her side, she knew she wouldn't face it alone. As for the Dragon Hunter, a flicker of curiosity sparked within her. His actions, defying the Council to help them, were a puzzle she intended to solve. But for now, there were more pressing matters at hand.

With a deep breath, Saraphina focused her remaining energy. The air shimmered around her, and with a powerful surge, she took flight. Elian clung to her neck, his fear replaced by a sense of awe as the world shrank beneath them. Iroh, nestled securely on her back, remained unconscious. But in her other arm, the Dragon Hunter stirred slightly. She glanced down at him, a flicker of gratitude softening her gaze.

"We're going home," she whispered, her voice barely audible over the wind. Home to the hidden village nestled within the mountains, a place of refuge for those ostracized by the Council. A place where they could heal, regroup, and plan for the future. The embers of rebellion had been ignited, and Saraphina, the Dragon Shifter reborn from the flames, carried them with her, a beacon of hope for a world where dragons and humans could coexist.

Chapter 15: The Price of Victory

As Saraphina, Elian, and Iroh visited the village, what awaited them left all of them distraught. The village had been laid to ruin, and flames burned bright as if someone had attacked it.

Saraphina's heart sank as she descended toward the village, the weight of despair settling heavily in her chest. The once serene haven now lay in ruins, charred remnants of buildings scattered amidst billowing smoke. Flames flickered wildly, licking hungrily at what remained of the structures.

Elian's grip tightened around Saraphina's neck, his eyes wide with horror as he took in the devastation below. "What... what happened?" he choked out, his voice trembling with disbelief.

Saraphina landed gently amidst the chaos, her mind racing as she scanned the scene for any sign of life. Iroh stirred on her back, groaning softly as he regained consciousness. With a gentle touch, she eased him down to the ground, her eyes never leaving the destruction before her.

The Dragon Hunter, still weak from his injuries, struggled to sit up, his gaze flickering with a mixture of confusion and concern. "This wasn't supposed to happen," he muttered, his voice hoarse with emotion.

Saraphina's jaw clenched as she took in the devastation, her fists tightening at her sides. "Who would do this?" she whispered, her voice choked with emotion.

As they moved through the wreckage, searching for any survivors, a sense of dread settled over them like a suffocating blanket. The once bustling village was now eerily silent, the only sound the crackling of flames and the occasional creak of collapsing timber.

With a heavy heart, Saraphina approached her shed, the place where she had sought solace and found strength in the guidance of the Chief. But as she pushed open the door, her worst fears were realized.

There, sprawled on the floor, lay the Chief, his once vibrant spirit now dimmed in the pale light filtering through the wreckage. Saraphina's breath caught in her throat as she rushed to his side, dropping to her knees beside him.

She reached out a trembling hand, hoping against hope for any sign of life. But as her fingers brushed against his cold skin, she felt the crushing weight of despair settle over her like a suffocating fog. The Chief was gone, his life extinguished like a candle in the wind.

Tears welled in Saraphina's eyes as she cradled the Chief's lifeless form, her heart breaking with the enormity of their loss. Elian stood beside her, his own eyes brimming with unshed tears as he watched helplessly, his heart aching for the pain his friend was enduring.

"Saraphina," he whispered, his voice choked with emotion. "I'm so sorry."

But there were no words to ease the agony that gripped her soul, no comfort to be found in the wake of such devastation. With a strangled cry, Saraphina buried her face in the Chief's chest, her tears mingling with the blood that stained his robes.

At that moment, all she could feel was the crushing weight of grief, a tidal wave of sorrow threatening to consume her whole. As she clung to the Chief's lifeless body, her world shattered into a million jagged pieces, leaving her adrift in a sea of pain and loss.

***

Elian held Saraphina close, his arms a shelter from the storm of grief raging within her. He could feel her body tremble with each sob, her tears soaking into the fabric of his shirt as she clung to him as if he were her lifeline in the midst of a tumultuous sea.

Iroh and the Dragon Hunter stood nearby, their expressions a mixture of sympathy and helplessness as they watched Saraphina's anguish unfold before them. Iroh's brow furrowed with concern, his heart heavy with the weight of their collective loss. The Dragon Hunter, too, felt a pang of guilt gnaw at his conscience, knowing that his actions had inadvertently led to this tragedy.

But for Saraphina, the world had narrowed to the confines of Elian's embrace, her thoughts consumed by the relentless refrain of self-blame that echoed in the depths of her soul. In her mind, every failure, every misstep, every loss was a testament to her own inadequacy, a damning indictment of her worth as a leader and as a friend.

"It's all my fault," she whispered hoarsely, her voice choked with anguish. "I should have been stronger; I should have protected them. But I failed... I failed them all."

Elian's heart clenched at her words, the raw pain in her voice cutting him to the core. He held her tighter, his own eyes stinging with unshed tears as he struggled to find the words to offer her solace.

"No, Saraphina," he murmured softly, his voice trembling with emotion. "You did everything you could. None of this is your fault. We're in this together, remember? We'll find a way through this, I promise."

But Saraphina could find no comfort in his words, no respite from the relentless onslaught of guilt that threatened to consume her whole. At that moment, all she could do was surrender to the overwhelming tide of sorrow that threatened to engulf her, clinging to Elian as if he were the only anchor keeping her from being swept away.

As Saraphina's sobs began to subside into quiet hiccups, she lifted her head from Elian's chest, her eyes red-rimmed and swollen with tears. She turned her gaze toward the Dragon Hunter, his words piercing through the haze of her grief with unexpected clarity.

"This is what always happens…"

"What do you mean?" Saraphina looked at him as she wiped her eyes.

"The Council's heinous atrocities have caused destruction in Draconia for more than a century now…." the Dragon Hunter responded.

"What?" she repeated, her voice soft with disbelief. "But how..."

The Dragon Hunter nodded solemnly, his expression grave. "Yes," he confirmed, his voice tinged with bitterness. "I was sealed away, imprisoned in the depths of time until I was awoken by the chaos that now grips this world. And when I emerged, I saw the truth of what had become of Draconia."

He paced restlessly, his movements agitated as he recounted the centuries of corruption and animosity that had festered within the heart of their once proud civilization. "The Council, with their greed and their power-hungry ambitions, they brought about their own downfall," he spat, his words laced with venom. "They turned brother against brother, sister against sister until all that remained was chaos and destruction."

Saraphina listened in stunned silence, her mind reeling at the revelation of the Dragon Hunter's centuries-long slumber. And as she pieced together the fragments of his story, a flicker of understanding began to dawn within her.

"So, you sought to destroy Draconia as retribution for their sins," she murmured, her voice tinged with sorrow.

The Dragon Hunter nodded grimly. "Yes," he admitted, his gaze dark and haunted. "But now, I see that vengeance is not the answer. The cycle of violence only begets more pain and suffering. We must find another way, a way to rebuild and heal the wounds of the past."

Saraphina's heart clenched at his words, a glimmer of hope stirring within her battered soul. Perhaps, amidst the ashes of their broken world, there was still a chance for redemption, for forgiveness, for a future where dragons and humans could coexist in harmony once more.

But as she glanced around at the ruins of their once peaceful village, the road ahead seemed daunting and uncertain. Yet, with

Elian by her side and the unlikely alliance forged with the Dragon Hunter, Saraphina knew that they would face whatever trials lay ahead together, drawing strength from each other as they embarked on a journey to rebuild what had been lost and forge a new path forward.

"There might be a way to fix all of this," Iroh's words sparked a glimmer of hope amidst the despair that hung heavy in the air. Saraphina's gaze flickered toward him, her eyes brightening with newfound determination.

"The Mountain of Peace," she repeated, her voice tinged with excitement. "If the Elder Dragons dwell there, then perhaps there is still a chance to restore Draconia to its former glory."

Elian nodded in agreement, his expression hopeful. "It's worth a try," he said, his voice steady despite the uncertainty that lay ahead. "If anyone can reason with the Elder Dragons, it's you, Saraphina."

Saraphina's heart swelled with gratitude at Elian's words, his unwavering faith in her bolstering her resolve. With a determined nod, she turned toward the Dragon Hunter, her eyes meeting his with newfound conviction.

"We need your help," she said, her voice firm. "Together, we can journey to the Mountain of Peace and seek an audience with the Elder Dragons. With their guidance, perhaps we can find a way to heal the wounds that divide our world."

Elian wrapped his arms around Saraphina, offering her a reassuring embrace as she leaned into him, drawing strength from his comforting presence.

"We'll make sure everything goes well, Saraphina," he murmured softly, his voice filled with unwavering confidence. "Together, we'll find a way through this."

Saraphina nodded against his chest, her heart heavy with the weight of responsibility but also buoyed by the support of her friends. With a deep breath, she straightened, her resolve renewed as she turned to face Iroh.

"Iroh," she said, her voice steady despite the turmoil within her. "Lead us to the Mountain of Peace. We must seek out the Elder Dragons and plead our case."

Iroh met her gaze with a solemn nod, his eyes reflecting the same determination that burned within her own. "Of course, Saraphina," he replied, his voice steady with resolve. "I will guide us there."

But before they could set out on their journey, the Dragon Hunter stepped forward, his expression serious as he addressed them.

"I will accompany you," he insisted, his tone brooking no argument. "If we are to have any hope of convincing the Elder Dragons to aid us, they must see that I am committed to this cause as well."

Saraphina regarded him for a moment, weighing his words carefully. Despite the mistrust that lingered between them, she couldn't deny the logic of his argument. If they were to have any chance of success, they would need all the help they could get.

"Very well," she agreed, at last, her voice firm. "But remember, Dragon Hunter, our trust is not easily earned. You will need to prove yourself if you wish to be a part of this journey."

The Dragon Hunter inclined his head in acknowledgment, a hint of determination glinting in his eyes. "I understand," he said simply.

With an unlikely alliance forged and their path set before them, Saraphina, Elian, Iroh, and the Dragon Hunter set out toward the north, their hearts filled with hope and determination as they embarked on a journey that would shape the fate of their world.

Chapter 16: A New Dawn

The journey to the Mountain of Peace was not an easy one. As Saraphina, Elian, Iroh, and the Dragon Hunter ventured forth, they encountered rugged terrain, treacherous obstacles, and unforeseen challenges at every turn. However, together, they faced each trial with courage and determination, their bond growing stronger with each step they took.

Saraphina and Elian walked hand in hand, drawing strength from each other as they navigated the rocky paths and winding trails that led them ever closer to their destination. Despite the hardships they faced, they refused to falter, their spirits buoyed by the knowledge that they were not alone in their quest.

Iroh led the way, his keen instincts guiding them through the wilderness with the skill of a seasoned navigator. His knowledge of the land proved invaluable as he charted a course through the dense forests, steep cliffs, and rushing rivers that lay in their path.

Trailing behind them, the Dragon Hunter watched with a mixture of awe and admiration as Saraphina and her companions forged ahead, undaunted by the trials that lay before them. Despite his own doubts and reservations, he found himself drawn to their unwavering resolve, inspired by their courage in the face of adversity.

As they journeyed onward, they encountered breathtaking vistas and awe-inspiring landscapes that filled them with wonder and amazement. Each new sight served as a reminder of the beauty and majesty of the world they fought to protect, fueling their determination to succeed in their quest.

Amidst the beauty, they also encountered danger and hardship. They battled fierce storms, fierce beasts, and unseen perils that tested their strength and resolve to the limit. Yet through it all, they stood together, united in their purpose and unwavering in their determination to reach their goal.

As they pressed on, drawing ever closer to the Mountain of Peace, they knew their journey was far from over. But with Saraphina and Elian leading the way and Iroh and the Dragon Hunter by their side, they faced the challenges in their path with hope in their hearts and courage in their souls, knowing that together, they could overcome anything that the world threw their way.

As the weary travelers settled by the banks of a serene river, the rushing waters providing a soothing soundtrack to their momentary respite, Iroh turned to the Dragon Hunter with a curious expression.

"Forgive me for not asking sooner," Iroh began, his voice gentle, "but what is your name?"

The Dragon Hunter's gaze flickered with a hint of surprise at the question as if he hadn't expected anyone to show interest in something as seemingly insignificant as his name. But after a moment's hesitation, he inclined his head in acknowledgment.

"My name..." he trailed off as if the words carried a weight of memories long forgotten. "My name is Draven."

Saraphina and Elian exchanged a glance, intrigued by the revelation. "Draven," Saraphina repeated softly, testing the name on her tongue as if savoring its taste.

Iroh nodded thoughtfully, his curiosity piqued. "A noble name," he remarked. "Does it hold any significance?"

Draven's expression grew somber as he turned his gaze toward the distant horizon, his thoughts drifting back to a time long past. "In another life, perhaps," he said quietly. "Once, I was born into a royal lineage of Dragon Shifters, destined for greatness. But my ability to transform brought only scorn and rejection from those who should have embraced me."

He paused, a haunted look in his eyes as he recounted the painful memories of his past. "I was cast out, forced to wander the world alone, a pariah among my own kind. And so, I became the Dragon Hunter, a name whispered in fear and awe by those who dared to defy me."

Saraphina's heart ached at the sadness in Draven's voice, the weight of his past sins bearing heavily upon him. "You don't have to be defined by your past, Draven," she said gently, extending a hand in a gesture of compassion. "We all have our scars; what matters is how we choose to heal them."

Draven regarded her with a mixture of surprise and gratitude, as if her words had struck a chord deep within his wounded soul.

As the fire crackled softly, casting dancing shadows across the faces of the weary travelers, Draven's voice grew quiet. His words were weighed down by the burden of memory.

"It was a night like any other," he began, his voice hollow with grief. "My family, proud descendants of the ancient Dragon Shifters, lived in a secluded village nestled deep within the mountains. We lived in harmony with the land, guided by the wisdom of our ancestors and the teachings of the Elder Dragons."

"But that harmony was shattered one fateful night," Draven continued, his voice trembling with emotion. "The Council of Dragons, blinded by their thirst for power and control, descended upon our village like a storm unleashed. They accused us of heresy, of defying their authority, and in their rage, they unleashed their fury upon us."

Tears welled in Draven's eyes as he recounted the horrors of that night, the screams of his loved ones echoing in his ears like a haunting melody. "They slaughtered them without mercy," he whispered, his voice choked with anguish. "My parents, my siblings, all gone in an instant. Their lives were snuffed out by the cruelty of those who should have protected them."

Saraphina's heart clenched at the pain in Draven's voice, the magnitude of his loss too great to comprehend. She reached out to him, her touch a silent gesture of solidarity and support.

"I'm so sorry, Draven," she murmured, her voice filled with empathy. "No one should have to endure such senseless violence."

Draven nodded, his gaze distant as he relived the nightmare of that tragic night. "Their blood stains my hands," he whispered, his voice barely audible above the crackling of the fire. "It's a burden I fear I'll carry with me until the end of my days."

Saraphina listened intently as Draven's tale unfolded, her heart heavy with sorrow at the tragedy that had befallen him. But before Saraphina could offer reassurance, Draven's expression hardened, his eyes flashing with a steely resolve.

"The corruption of this world," he interjected, his voice tinged with bitterness, "it's what led to the massacre of my family, the betrayal of everything I once held dear. That is what drove me to embrace the darkness within me, to become the very thing I once despised."

Saraphina's heart ached at the weight of his words; the depth of his anguish laid bare before her. She could see the pain etched in the lines of his face, the haunted look in his eyes betraying the turmoil that raged within his soul.

"But that darkness does not define you, Draven," she insisted, her voice gentle but firm. "You still have a choice, a chance to make amends for the sins of your past. Together, we can forge a new path, one of redemption and hope."

Draven regarded her with a mixture of disbelief and longing as if her words had awakened a glimmer of hope within him that he had long thought extinguished.

"Do you truly believe that?" he asked, his voice barely above a whisper.

Saraphina met his gaze with unwavering certainty. "I do," she affirmed, her voice filled with conviction. "And I will stand by your side every step of the way."

At that moment, amidst the tranquil beauty of the riverbank, a flicker of hope ignited within Draven's heart, a beacon of light in the darkness that had consumed him for so long. With Saraphina's steadfast support and the unwavering friendship of his companions, perhaps there was still a chance for him to find redemption and reclaim the light that had been lost to him.

***

As they made their way toward the towering peaks of the Mountain of Peace, Saraphina, Elian, Iroh, and Draven embraced their true forms, their bodies shimmering with the ancient power of the Dragon Shifters. With each beat of their wings, they soared through the crisp mountain air, their hearts filled with a sense of purpose and determination.

As they journeyed through the dense forests and winding valleys surrounding the mountain, they encountered a myriad of creatures, from majestic deer to playful foxes, each one a testament to the beauty and diversity of the natural world. Yet amidst the tranquility of their surroundings, a sense of urgency gnawed at the edges of their consciousness, driving them ever onward toward their ultimate goal.

At last, after days of arduous travel and countless trials, they reached the summit of the Mountain of Peace. As they stood atop the windswept peak, their eyes gazed out upon a breathtaking panorama of snow-capped peaks and rolling clouds, the world stretching out before them in all its untamed splendor.

However, amidst the awe-inspiring beauty that surrounded them, there was also a palpable sense of anticipation, a feeling that they had finally arrived at a place of great significance. For here, amidst the towering heights of the mountain, lay the domain of the Elder Dragons, ancient beings of wisdom and power whose guidance could tip the scales in their favor.

With hearts pounding in anticipation, Saraphina and her companions approached the entrance to the Elder Dragons' lair, their footsteps echoing softly against the rugged terrain. As they entered the cavernous depths, they were met with a sense of reverence and awe, their eyes drawn to the shimmering forms of the Elder Dragons who lay within.

The Elder Dragons regarded them with eyes that seemed to pierce to the very depths of their souls, their ancient wisdom etched in the lines of their weathered faces. As Saraphina stepped forward, her voice filled with quiet determination, she knew that their journey was far from over.

"We seek your guidance, mighty Elder Dragons," she announced, her words echoing through the cavern like a prayer. "We come seeking justice for the injustices that have been committed against us and hope for a future where peace and harmony can reign once more."

As the echoes of Saraphina's words faded into the cavernous depths of the Elder Dragons' lair, a hushed silence descended upon the chamber, the air thick with anticipation. Saraphina and her companions waited with bated breath, their eyes fixed on the ancient beings before them, hoping for a sign of acknowledgment or guidance.

But before the Elder Dragons could respond, a sudden disturbance shattered the tranquility of the moment. A figure emerged from the shadows, his presence casting a dark shadow over the gathering. It was Veridan, the head of the Council of Dragons, his regal form exuding an aura of authority and power.

"Saraphina," Veridan intoned, his voice dripping with disdain. "What a surprise to see you here, consorting with traitors and outcasts. Have you come to beg for forgiveness or perhaps to plead for mercy?"

Saraphina's jaw clenched at the venom in Veridan's words, her eyes narrowing with determination. "We have come seeking justice," she replied, her voice steady despite the anger simmering beneath the surface. "Justice for the atrocities committed by the Council of Dragons and for the suffering inflicted upon innocent lives."

Veridan scoffed, a cruel smirk twisting his lips. "Innocent lives?" he mocked. "There are no innocents in this world, only those who are too weak to seize power for themselves. And as for justice, it is a fleeting illusion, a fantasy concocted by fools who cling to false hope."

Saraphina's hands curled into fists at her sides, her resolve hardening with each word spoken by the corrupt council leader. "You will answer for your crimes, Veridan!" she vowed, her voice ringing with conviction. "The Elder Dragons will see the truth of your actions, and justice will be served."

But Veridan only laughed, the sound echoing through the chamber like the tolling of a funeral bell. "The Elder Dragons?" he sneered. "They are relics of a bygone era, their wisdom nothing more than a fading memory. You would do well to remember that, Saraphina, before you find yourself on the wrong side of history."

With a contemptuous glance toward Saraphina and her companions, Veridan turned on his heel and disappeared into the shadows, leaving behind a palpable sense of unease and uncertainty in his wake.

Saraphina and her companions exchanged a tense glance, the weight of Veridan's words hanging heavy in the air. But amidst the darkness that threatened to engulf them, a flicker of determination burned bright within their hearts, a reminder that their quest for justice and redemption was far from over. With the guidance of the Elder Dragons, they would continue to fight for a future where peace and harmony could reign once more.

Chapter 17: Love Conquers All

The chamber erupted into chaos as Veridan's contemptuous dismissal ignited the spark of conflict. With a flourish of his cloak, shadows swirled around him, coalescing into sinister forms that took the shape of dark dragons. Saraphina and Draven, knowing what they faced, didn't hesitate. They embraced their true forms, their bodies shifting and contorting until they stood as majestic dragons, ready to defend their cause.

The clash of scales and claws reverberated through the chamber as Saraphina and Draven lunged forward, meeting the dark dragons head-on. With every swipe and roar, they fought fiercely, their determination matched only by the ferocity of their adversaries.

Meanwhile, Elian swiftly guided Iroh to safety, leading him into a hidden alcove away from the fray. Though his heart raced with fear, Elian knew that protecting Iroh was paramount, even as the sounds of battle echoed around them.

Above, the Elder Dragons observed, their ancient eyes gleaming with a mixture of concern and determination. Though they could not intervene directly, their presence lent strength to Saraphina and her companions, a silent assurance that they were not alone in their struggle.

As the battle raged on, each blow struck and parried, Saraphina and Draven found themselves pushed to their limits. But with unwavering resolve, they pressed on, fueled by the knowledge that their cause was just and their determination unyielding.

Veridan's mocking laughter still echoed in the chamber as Saraphina and Draven stood ready to confront the dark dragons conjured by their adversary. Saraphina's eyes blazed with determination as she locked gazes with Veridan, his voice cutting through the chaos.

"Saraphina," Veridan sneered, his tone dripping with disdain. "Do you truly believe you can stand against me? Against the might of darkness itself?"

Saraphina's jaw clenched, her resolve unwavering. "I believe in justice, Veridan. And I will not let your darkness consume this realm any longer."

With a flick of his wrist, Veridan commanded the dark dragons to attack, their snarls filling the air as they lunged toward Saraphina and Draven. But Saraphina met their onslaught head-on, her claws meeting theirs with a resounding clash.

As the battle raged, Veridan's voice cut through the chaos once more, taunting Saraphina with cruel words. "You cling to the past, Saraphina, to the fading light of the Elder Dragons. But their power is nothing compared to mine. You are fighting a losing battle."

Saraphina's eyes blazed with fury as she fought on, her voice defiant. "The Elder Dragons may be ancient, but their wisdom endures. And with their guidance, we will prevail."

Veridan's laughter echoed through the chamber once more, but it was tinged with frustration as Saraphina and Draven pushed back against the dark dragons with renewed ferocity. "You are a fool, Saraphina!" he spat. "But perhaps a fool with some semblance of power. Nevertheless, you will not stop me."

But Saraphina remained undeterred; her resolve unwavering as she fought alongside Draven, their determination shining brightly amidst the darkness. As the battle raged on, it became clear that Veridan's arrogance had blinded him to the strength of Saraphina's convictions, and no matter how fierce his darkness, it could never extinguish the light of justice burning within her heart.

As the battle raged on, Draven found himself momentarily overwhelmed by the sheer ferocity of the dark dragons' onslaught. Just as it seemed he might falter, Saraphina unleashed her Mighty Blazing Form, a radiant display of power that engulfed the chamber in a dazzling inferno.

Draven watched in awe as Saraphina's flames consumed the dark dragons, their shadows fading into nothingness before her might. The intensity of her transformation left him stunned, her flames burning brighter and more potent than anything he had ever witnessed.

With the dark dragons vanquished, Saraphina turned her blazing gaze toward Veridan, her roar echoing with righteous fury. "Veridan!" she thundered, her voice carrying the weight of her resolve. "This ends now. Surrender, or face the consequences of your actions."

But Veridan's response was not one of submission. With a snarl of defiance, he, too, underwent a transformation. His form twisted and contorted into a dark animosity that mirrored the shadows he had summoned.

Draven's heart sank as he beheld Veridan's transformation, the darkness within him manifesting in a tangible, malevolent form. He knew that the battle ahead would be fraught with danger, but he also knew that he could not falter in the face of such darkness.

Together, he and Saraphina braced themselves for the confrontation to come, their determination unyielding even in the face of Veridan's newfound power. As the chamber trembled with the tension of their impending clash, Draven knew that their fight was far from over and that the true test of their strength and resolve lay just ahead.

As the battle between Saraphina and Veridan raged on, the air crackled with raw energy, each blow exchanged echoing through the chamber like thunder. But despite her fierce determination, Saraphina found herself slowly succumbing to the insidious darkness of Veridan's attacks.

With every strike, Veridan's words cut deeper, his taunts and accusations striking at the very core of Saraphina's being. Doubt crept into her mind, fueled by Veridan's relentless onslaught of emotional manipulation.

"Saraphina," Veridan hissed, his voice laced with malice. "Do you truly believe that you fight for justice? Or are you merely a pawn in Elian's game, blinded by his lies and deceit?"

Saraphina's heart clenched at the mention of Elian, the seed of doubt planted by Veridan's words taking root in her mind. She glanced toward where Elian, who had taken Iroh to safety, uncertainty flickering in her eyes.

"And what of Iroh?" Veridan continued, his words like poison in Saraphina's ears. "Do you truly believe he is on your side? Or has he been playing you all along, biding his time until he can strike against you and claim victory for himself?"

Saraphina's breath caught in her throat, torn between the bonds of trust she had formed and the doubt Veridan's words now sowed within her. Her gaze flickered toward where Elian stood, her mind racing with uncertainty.

But it was Veridan's final accusation that struck the deepest of all. "And Draven," he sneered, his voice dripping with venom. "Do you not remember what he did? How he betrayed you, how he killed your parents in cold blood?"

Saraphina's world shattered at Veridan's words, her mind reeling with the weight of his accusations. Memories long buried surged to the surface, conflicting emotions threatening to consume her.

In a moment of desperation, Saraphina reached for the light within her but instead found herself ensnared by the darkness that Veridan had cultivated. With a cry of anguish, she broke free from the shackles of doubt but, in doing so, lost control.

Her powers surged uncontrollably, lashing out in every direction as she grappled with the darkness that threatened to consume her. The chamber trembled with the force of her unleashed power, the very fabric of reality warping and distorting under its weight.

As Saraphina's uncontrollable rampage engulfed the chamber, chaos reigned supreme. Her attacks spared none, striking out indiscriminately at friend and foe alike. Draven, the Elder Dragons, and even Iroh found themselves in the path of her destructive fury.

But as Saraphina's fury threatened to consume everything in its path, a figure stepped forward, unwavering in the face of her rage. It was Elian, her husband, his gaze steady and unwavering as he met her feral growl with a calm resolve.

"Saraphina," Elian's voice cut through the chaos, his words a beacon of clarity amidst the storm. "Remember who you are. Remember the bonds that tie us together."

Saraphina's growl faltered, uncertainty flickering in her eyes as she beheld the man standing before her. Memories flooded back, fragments of a life shared, of promises made and vows sworn.

Elian stepped closer, his hand outstretched in a gesture of peace. "We are married, Saraphina," he reminded her, his voice gentle yet firm. "We swore to protect Draconia together, no matter the cost. Everything will be fine, my love. Trust in our bond."

Saraphina's growl softened, the fire in her eyes dimming as she looked upon Elian, her husband, her rock amidst the tempest of her emotions. Slowly, the storm within her began to abate, the tumultuous rage giving way to a sense of clarity and calm.

With a deep breath, Saraphina allowed herself to be enveloped by Elian's embrace, the weight of their shared history grounding her in reality once more. At that moment, she knew that no matter what trials they faced, as long as they stood together, they would overcome them.

With Elian by her side, Saraphina turned away from the chaos she had wrought, her heart heavy with remorse yet filled with newfound determination. Though the scars of her rampage would linger, she knew that with the strength of their love and the bonds of their marriage, they would face whatever challenges lay ahead, united in their quest to protect Draconia at all costs.

As Saraphina transformed back into her human form, the weight of her actions crashing down upon her, she found solace in Elian's comforting embrace. Tears streamed down her cheeks as she clung to him, the release of her pent-up emotions overwhelming her.

Elian held her close, offering silent support as she wept, his own heart heavy with the weight of their shared ordeal. Together, they found a moment of respite amidst the chaos, drawing strength from each other's presence as they began to heal the wounds left by the battle.

As Saraphina and Elian held each other close, Draven and Iroh approached; their expressions a mixture of relief and exhaustion. With a shared sigh of happiness, they joined the embrace, finding comfort in the knowledge that their trials were finally over.

The chamber was bathed in a profound sense of peace as they stood together, the echoes of their victory mingling with the fading remnants of Veridan's darkness. In the end, justice had prevailed, and Veridan's malevolent presence disintegrated into the shadows from whence it came, vanquished by the collective strength and determination of those who stood against him.

As they looked upon the remnants of the battle, Saraphina felt a sense of closure wash over her, and the weight of her burdens finally lifted. Though scars remained, both physical and emotional, she knew that they would heal in time, their bonds forged stronger than ever in the crucible of adversity.

With Elian's hand in hers and her companions by her side, Saraphina turned toward the future with renewed hope and determination. Whatever challenges awaited them, they would face them together, united in their resolve to protect Draconia and ensure peace and harmony reigned once more.

***

Guided by the wisdom of the Elder Dragons, Saraphina, Elian, and Draven embarked on their journey to rebuild Draconia from the ashes of Veridan's tyranny. Together, they worked tirelessly to mend the wounds inflicted upon their homeland, their determination unwavering in the face of adversity.

As the days turned into weeks and the weeks into months, their efforts began to bear fruit. With Draven's newfound leadership and the unwavering support of the people, a new government was established, one founded upon principles of justice, equality, and unity.

Under Draven's guidance, Draconia flourished once more, its scars fading into the annals of history as the land reclaimed its former glory. The people looked to Saraphina and Elian as their saviors, their names spoken with reverence and gratitude for the sacrifices they had made.

But amidst the celebrations and triumphs, there came moments of sorrow. Iroh, the faithful companion who had stood by their side through countless trials, eventually passed away, his spirit ascending to join the ranks of the Elder Dragons.

Saraphina paid her kindest respects at Iroh's grave, her heart heavy with grief yet filled with gratitude for the time they had shared. She knew that his legacy would live on in the hearts of those who had loved him, a beacon of loyalty and friendship that would never be forgotten.

As the years passed, Saraphina and Elian's deeds became the stuff of legend, their names solidifying a special place in time as the saviors of Draconia. Though their adventures had come to an end, their legacy endured, a testament to the power of courage, compassion, and unwavering determination.

And so, the day was saved, not by the might of armies or the clang of swords, but by the bravery and resilience of a few individuals who dared to dream of a better world. And in their triumph, Draconia found hope, unity, and a future filled with promise.

In the heart of Draconia, amidst the tranquil beauty of the land they had fought so hard to protect, Saraphina and Elian found peace. Their days were filled with quiet moments of joy, surrounded by the love and admiration of their people.

As they looked out upon the kingdom they had helped rebuild, Saraphina and Elian understood that love had been the guiding force that had carried them through the darkest of times. It was love that had bound them together, love that had given them the strength to persevere, and love that had ultimately conquered all.

In each other's arms, they found solace and strength, knowing that no matter what trials lay ahead, they would face them together. As they watched the sunset over the horizon, casting a golden glow upon the land they called home, Saraphina and Elian knew that their love would endure for all eternity, a beacon of hope in a world filled with darkness.

www.ingramcontent.com/pod-product-compliance
Lightning Source LLC
Chambersburg PA
CBHW061257120726
48001CB00001B/351